PENGUIN CLASSICS

THE IMMORALIST

André Paul Guillaume Gide was born in Paris on 22 November 1869. His father, who died when he was eleven, was Professor of Law at the Sorbonne. An only child, Gide had an irregular and lonely upbringing and was educated in a Protestant secondary school in Paris and privately. He became devoted to literature and music, began his literary career as an essayist, and then went on to poetry, biography, fiction, drama, criticism, reminiscence and translation. By 1917 he had emerged as a prophet to French youth and his unorthodox views were a source of endless debate and attack. In 1947 he was awarded the Nobel Prize for Literature and in 1948, as a distinguished foreigner, was given an honorary degree at Oxford. He married his cousin in 1895; he died in Paris in 1951 at the age of eighty-one.

Among Gide's best-known works in England are *Strait is the Gate* (*La Porte étroite*), the first novel he wrote, which was published in France in 1909; *la Symphonie pastorale*, 1919; *The Immoralist* (*L'Immoraliste*), 1902; *The Counterfeiters* (*Les Faux-Monnayeurs*), published in 1926; and the famous *Journals* covering his life from 1889 to 1949 and published originally in four volumes.

E. M. Forster said of him: 'The humanist has four leading characteristics – curiosity, a free mind, belief in good taste, and a belief in the human race – and all four are present in Gide . . . the humanist of our age.'

David Watson read Modern and Medieval Languages at Cambridge University and studied for his Ph.D. at Manchester. He is the author of *Paradox and Desire in Samuel Beckett's Fiction* (1991). His previous translations from French include *The Butcher* and *Behind Closed Doors* by Alina Reyes; *The Proof* and *The Third Lie* by Agota Kristof; and the anonymous *Lila Says*. He lives in London.

Alan Sheridan read English at Cambridge University, then spent five years in Paris as assistant at the Lycées Henri IV and Condorcet. He is the author of *Michel Foucault: The Will to Truth* (1980) and of the biography *André Gide: A Life in the Present* (1998; Penguin, 2000). He has translated over fifty French books, including works by Sartre, Lacan and Foucault.

THE IMMORALIST

ANDRÉ GIDE

TRANSLATED BY DAVID WATSON

WITH AN INTRODUCTION BY ALAN SHERIDAN

PENGUIN BOOKS

PENGUIN BOOKS

Published by the Penguin Group

Penguin Group (USA) Inc., 375 Hudson Street, New York, New York 10014, U S.A.

Penguin Books Ltd, 80 Strand, London WC2R 0RL, England

Penguin Books Australia Ltd, 250 Camberwell Road, Camberwell, Victoria 3124, Australia

Penguin Books Canada Ltd, 10 Alcorn Avenue, Toronto, Ontario, Canada M4V 3B2

Penguin Books India (P) Ltd, 11 Community Centre, Panchsheel Park, New Delhi – 110 017, India

Penguin Group (NZ), cnr Airborne and Rosedale Roads, Albany, Auckland 1310, New Zealand

Penguin Books (South Africa) (Pty) Ltd, 24 Sturdee Avenue,
Rosebank, Johannesburg 2196, South Africa

Penguin Books Ltd, Registered Offices. 80 Strand, London WC2R 0RL, England

This translation first published in Penguin Books (UK) 2000
Published in Penguin Books (USA) 2001

7   9   10   8   6

Translation copyright © David Watson, 2000
Introduction copyright © Alan Sheridan, 2000
All rights reserved

LIBRARY OF CONGRESS CATALOGING IN PUBLICATION DATA
Gide, André, 1869-1951
[Immoraliste English]
The immoralist / André Gide ; translated by David Watson ,
with an introduction by Alan Sheridan.
p. cm.—(Penguin twentieth-century classics)
ISBN 0 14 21 8002 5 (pbk   alk paper)
I. Watson, David, 1959– II Title   III Series
PQ2613.I2 14813 2001
843¢ 912—dc21   2001032721

Printed in the United States of America
Set in Bembo

Introduction

'The best title for a book published here for years,' said Alfred Vallette when presented with the manuscript of *L'Immoraliste*. He sounds like a publisher with a nose for scandal – and sales. Even the most high-minded publisher is not averse to free publicity and large sales, of course, but Vallette could hardly have expected either from his authors. At the beginning of the twentieth century, publishers of literary works like Gide's were not what we understand by publishers. They were the owners of bookshops or literary reviews. Novels were often serialized first in the review, then published in volume form at the author's expense. Proust, for example, paid for the printing of the first volume of *À la recherche du temps perdu* and it was to be many years before Gide stopped paying for the printing of his books. Publishing at the turn of the century was an altogether more off-hand matter, too. There was no promotion, no army of sales reps, no foreign rights department. Proofs arrived a few weeks after the manuscript; publication followed a few weeks after that. In 1901 a now much chastened Gide ordered a printing of 300 copies for his new book. In this way he could avoid the embarrassment of hundreds of unsold copies: 'If twelve hundred were printed, the sales would seem four times worse and I'd suffer four times as much.' (He had had 1,650 copies of *Les Nourritures terrestres* – *Fruits of the Earth* – printed. After two years, 210 copies had been sold.)

The Immoralist did cause something of a scandal, though given its tiny circulation, rather among Gide's friends and acquaintances than among the public at large. Michel, the 'immoralist' of the title, is a desiccated young scholar, ignorant of both his sexual needs and the world in which he lives, a man whose interests do not go beyond 'ruins and books'. At the behest of his dying father, he marries Marceline, a young woman of similar interests: he scarcely knows her, but, he tells himself, he knows no other woman. He thinks of a wife as no more than a companion. During their long, unconsummated 'honeymoon' in North Africa, Michel comes close to death from tuberculosis. As he recovers, he begins to discover for the first time the beauties of the living world around him. More hesitantly, never entirely peeling away the layers of self-ignorance and self-delusion, he begins to discover his true sexual desires. The 'trigger' of Michel's recovery is a young Arab boy who has been befriended by his wife. Michel notes that he is like 'a graceful animal', that his body is 'completely naked beneath his thin white *gandourah*'. Back in Normandy, Michel becomes infatuated with his estate manager's seventeen-year-old son. Later, on a return trip to North Africa, Gide lets us know, with the discretion required at the time, that Michel is finally acting out his desires. In Naples, he wanders the streets at night: 'I touched things with my hand; I went prowling.'

The attraction of Gide's title for his publisher had probably less to do with the promise of titillating incidents than with its fashionable allusion to Nietzsche. The influence of the German philosopher on young French intellectuals was now at its zenith, rivalling that of Wagner. It is an influence that is apparent in Gide's *Le Voyage d'Urien* (1893), more evident in his *Le Prométhée mal enchaîné (Prometheus Misbound, 1899)*. Above all, *Les Nourritures terrestres* (1897) has only one literary model, Nietzsche's *Thus Spake Zarathustra*. If Michel is an 'immoralist' it is not because he finally succumbs to 'immorality': his sexual activities are incidental to the novel's main concern. Michel is an 'immoralist' because he has adopted Nietzsche's view that morality is a weapon of the weak, of a slave mentality. To become fully human, men must have the courage to kill the God that has infected the freedom of their will. There was, of course, a great deal more to Nietzsche's critique of Christianity and its effect on Western civilization than could be encapsulated in the much misunderstood notion of the *Übermensch*, the Superman.

The vehicle of the work's Nietzscheanism is Ménalque – his name, odd in a realistic novel, is the Gallicized version of Virgil's Menalchas (the French always Gallicize Greek and Latin names), and derives from his earlier incarnation in *Les Nourritures terrestres*. Indeed, the original germ of *L'Immoraliste* was the unpursued project of a *Life of Ménalque*. In the novel he is an altogether more rounded character than the shadowy presence of the earlier work. Ménalque is also a recognizably Wildean figure: he has Wilde's scorn of morality, his love of pleasure and travel, his homosexuality and, though he could hardly aspire to Wilde's wit, he is given to the odd epigram. He has even been the victim of 'an absurd, shameful lawsuit' that caused a great scandal and turned him into a social outcast. Gide first met Wilde in a Parisian literary salon in 1891. Wilde had not yet attained fame (the first of the great comedies, *Lady Windermere's Fan*, would be put on the following year), nor sunk to the depths of infamy (the trials were four years away). Wilde was then staying at the residence of the British Ambassador, Lord Lytton. For the puritanical twenty-two-year-old Gide, the encounter with Wilde was cataclysmic. For three weeks, they met every day. 'The man is admirable, admirable,' he wrote. Jules Renard noted in his *Journal*: 'Gide is in love with Oscar Wilde.' He was not in *love* with Wilde: he was simply shaken to his very foundations, his belief in Christian morality under threat and a new, terrifyingly attractive world opened up to view. The pages covering these weeks were torn out of Gide's journal, then, over the pages of his diary for 11 and 12 December, he wrote, in large letters, the single word WILDE. Retreating to the puritan heartland of his maternal grandmother's home in the south of France, removed from the hypnotic power of Wilde's physical presence, Gide wrote in his *Journal*: 'Lord, I have come back to Thee because I believe that all is vanity save knowing Thee . . . I have followed tortuous ways and thought to grow rich with false gods . . . I find myself poor indeed. Lord, save me from evil . . . Wilde has done me nothing but harm. When I was with him I forgot how to think . . .' In the summer of 1894 Gide bumped into Wilde and Lord Alfred Douglas in Florence, but the crucial meeting occurred the following winter in Algiers. One night, in a Moorish café, sensing Gide's attraction for a young Arab musician, Wilde acted as go-between to the extent of providing a room. 'Since then, whenever I have sought pleasure, it is the memory of that night that I have pursued,' Gide wrote twenty-five years later. By a curious coincidence, Nietzsche and Wilde died within months of one another in 1900, as Gide was writing *L'Immoraliste*.

As was usually the case with Gide, the writing was a slow, painful, often interrupted process. 'I have lived it for four years,' he wrote to Francis Jammes, 'and have written it to put it behind me. I suffer a book as one suffers an illness. I now respect only the books that all but kill their authors.' As usual, too, the book had existed in his head in some form long before he began to work on it – in this case for some fifteen years. The corollary of this is that he had several coexisting projects for works. Moreover, one of these would be conceived as a corrective to another, a compensatory swing of the creative pendulum in a man notoriously incapable of not seeing both sides of an argument. Thus *L'Immoraliste* was conceived as a critique of *Les Nourritures terrestres*, *La Porte étroite* (*Strait is the Gate*, 1909) as a reaction to *L'Immoraliste* and *Les Caves du Vatican* (*The Vatican Cellars*, 1914) as a delighted escape from the puritan world of *La Porte étroite*. Yet 'all these subjects developed in parallel, concurrently . . . If I could have done, I should have written them *together*' (*Journal*, 12 July 1914). Not only did 'the excess of one find a secret permission in the excess of the other and together establish a balance', but such a balance existed within each work. An inattentive reader might imagine that *L'Immoraliste* was an apologia for Nietzschean 'immoralism', *La Porte étroite* a nostalgic evocation of a lost world of moral simplicities. But in truth each is an implicit critique of its subject. Indeed, in the case of *L'Immoraliste* Gide was driven to write a preface to a second edition that made just this point: 'I no more wanted this book to be an accusation than an apology. I refrained from passing judgement.' Depending on one's own moral predispositions, one may well agree with Michel that 'Culture, which is born of life, ends up killing it', sympathize with a Michel who feels almost strangled by the made-to-measure moral clothes that he has now outworn, share his boredom with the world of Paris salons, delight in his discovery of the beauties of the natural world, even of his sexuality, but *L'Immoraliste* is not so much an apologia for Nietzschean ideas as an exploration of what can happen if such ideas fall into the hands of someone too weak to sustain them. As Michel himself puts it: 'Knowing how to free oneself is nothing; the difficult thing is knowing how to live with that freedom.' Marceline, Michel's wife, sees this very clearly: 'I understand your doctrine . . . but it leaves out the weak.' 'And so it should,' Michel retorts. It 'leaves out' Marceline and her child. It virtually does away with Michel himself: this supposed Nietzschean complains of his lack of will and is reduced to calling on his friends to get him out of his North African lethargy.

It was appropriate, if not inevitable, that a critique of that formless, or at least multiform, Nietzschean dithyramb, *Les Nourritures terrestres*, should take the form of a realistic novel. How else was an exemplum, a particular application of the theory, to be worked out in fictional terms? Yet for a number of reasons Gide was resistant to what is usually regarded as the novel form. So little was it a term that he used of his own work that he referred to *Les Faux-Monnayeurs* (*The Counterfeiters*, 1926) as his first (and, presumably, last) novel. Gide's literary beginnings were in the Symbolist movement, which saw the task of art as being to suggest the ineffable, Mallarmé's aspiration to the condition of music, rather than do anything so vulgar as represent what is popularly called 'reality'. Nietzsche helped Gide to move away from what he had come to regard as a metropolitan hothouse into the fresh air of nature. Yet bathing naked in sunlight or icy water, throwing off one's moral notions with one's clothes, was still best expressed in poetry – or in prose that aspired to the condition of poetry. Only when a further reaction set in did the realistic novel come into its own for Gide. As a writer, he had an aversion to the dominant nineteenth-century notion of the novel, with its third-person, omniscient narrator, spying into the deepest recesses of characters and societies – an aversion no doubt compounded by a conviction that he would be quite incapable of assuming the role of God in fiction. (As a reader, he had no such inhibitions: a good part of each day was spent in devouring the great French, English and Russian novels.) The solution adopted in almost all Gide's fiction is that of the first-person narrator, one by definition partial in viewpoint and possessed only of partial knowledge. The model used in many of these works is that of the classical *récit*. *Récit*, meaning, literally, an account of events, is one of a number of French terms used to describe what in English are called short stories. It obviously appealed to Gide as the most seemingly 'truthful' of the terms available (*conte*, tale, seems to suggest 'story-telling', lying). If the narrator speaks in the first person he can be held to account for the truth of his statements: a third-person narrator is obviously laying claim to knowledge that he does not have. With its sober, confessional character, this is a particularly suitable medium for material deriving directly from Gide's Protestant background. As if to reinforce the truth-telling nature of the narrative, Gide uses in his *récits* such devices as journals or documents arriving through the post. In *L'Immoraliste* Michel is too 'demoralized' to set pen to paper. Instead he summons his friends to his North African hide-out and *tells* them his story, which is written down by one of them and sent, with an accompanying letter, to his brother. *L'Immoraliste* is the first of the *récits*: the narrative line is spare, economic, the style unemphatic, of an elegant, deceptive simplicity. Here Gide eschews narrative prolixity and stylistic exuberance, characteristics that were left to another Gidean form, that of the *sotie*, or comic fantasy. It was not until *Les Caves du Vatican* of 1914 that Gide felt able to take on a third-person narrative of any length, though no doubt what made this possible for Gide was that this was a *sotie*, a type of work that replaces psychological motivation with coincidence, plausible narrative with the tall story and an omniscient narrator with one that we would now call 'unreliable'. Gide's greatest work, *Les Faux-Monnayeurs*, pursues this line, though even here the narrator admits limitations to his knowledge and is undermined by a second, first-person narrative, the journal of one of the characters.

To a greater or lesser degree works of literature derive from their authors' experiences, but few works of worth are *romans à clef*. As I have suggested, the *récits* have a very immediate connection with Gide's life, the *soties* much less so. *L'Immoraliste* examines the case of a man with wife and child, means and career, a man caught up therefore in a complicated network of overlapping relations and responsibilities, who comes to see his whole life as a hypocritical sham and, in pursuit of his true, authentic, homosexual self, abandons everything. This was, *in potentia*, at least, the central drama of Gide's own life. It must have come as no surprise to him that many readers identified him with his hero. Much of the indignation felt by certain readers towards Michel, Gide remarks in the Preface to the second edition, 'spilled over . . . on to me . . . I was all but confused with him'. Gide's aesthetic problem, the problem that had to be solved in terms of the work, was how the work could draw on, draw life from, the drama of his own life, while acquiring an autonomy, a difference, without which it could not grow into a work of art. There was also a personal problem here: for reasons connected with his own life, he could not afford to allow too obvious an identification between character and author. At its simplest, he solved this by a series of changes between the fictional and the autobiographical, sometimes involving simple reversal. Thus Michel is an academic (not a writer). His mother (not his father) dies during his childhood. His wife Marceline is beautiful and fair, and of a Catholic background (Madeleine Gide was rather plain and dark, and a Protestant). The route taken by Michel and Marceline on their honeymoon, and many of the events that take place then, come not from the Gides' honeymoon, but from an earlier trip to North Africa, etc. But the great, overriding difference between character and author lies in the ways in which they confront their similar problem. Michel takes Nietzsche simplistically, abandoning Culture for Nature, letting the weak go to the wall, and in the end losing everything. Gide knew what to leave as well as what to take of Nietzsche – and when to keep Nietzsche within the bounds of his (Gide's and Nietzsche's) books. While pursuing his natural inclinations, Gide cherished and retained his wife, his independent means (the means of his independence) and his professional position. In working out a modus vivendi that could accommodate both his marriage and his homosexual adventures, he called on the un-Nietzschean but very Gidean quality of compromise.

On the whole, the reviews were favourable, which is hardly surprising since most of them were written by friends; one of the reviewers (Henri Ghéon) was not only a friend but the book's dedicatee, another (Marcel Drouin) the author's brother-in-law and principal adviser on matters Nietzschean. Gide's new, spare, classical style won universal praise. 'A style of clarity and simplicity, elegant, yet strong, such as was practised in the seventeenth and eighteenth centuries' (Edmond Picard). Even those who complained of other things complimented the writing. Robert Scheffer praised 'the burning beauty of this prose' and the dazzling descriptions of the contrasting scenery of North Africa and Normandy. Like many others, he was perplexed by the title and its implied Nietzscheanism: 'Immoralist? Egotist rather.' Michel not only loses a fortune in childish pursuits, but sacrifices his wife to 'indescribable adventures'. Some, like Georges Rency, saw the book as an advocacy of Nietzscheanism. When reading it, 'one becomes bored with what one is, being where one is. One would like to set off, leave everything behind, one's family, one's country, one's habits, one's clothes, one's morality. One feels that one is also a bit of an immoralist. But one soon comes to one's senses . . .' One then realizes the damage that such a philosophy can do to others, not to speak of oneself. However, M. Rency, apparently unaware that the book itself amounts to a critique of such a philosophy, concluded that, despite this weakness at the heart of the work, André Gide was an interesting writer. Gide's friend Francis Vielé-Griffin took the opposite view: the book was 'the implicit apologia for the necessity of morality', which was simply the codification of the accumulated experience of generations attempting to create 'human sociability'.

Striking a Gidean equilibrium, Lucie Delarue-Mardrus, poet and wife of the eminent translator of *The Thousand and One Nights*, saw Michel as a case not so much of 'immoralism' as of 'an effort towards immoralism', someone so shaped by education that he seeks lessons from all and sundry, 'even young Arabs and wily Norman peasants', taking their 'crude ignorance' for 'primitive beauty' – one of those hopeless intellectuals who imagine that they have to *learn* to be spontaneous and natural. One of the most perceptive reviews was signed 'A. M. de Saint-Hubert', a name unknown to Gide. It began by pointing out the dangers of over-hasty, over-schematic interpretations. Like all works of art (and people), *L'Immoraliste* 'preserves its fluid outlines and remains unsusceptible to formulas; it may yield therefore to the most divergent interpretations.' Rency, for example, this reviewer went on to say, seemed to believe that the character of Michel could be confined within a few theoretical comments at the end of the book, which ignored the degree to which a work eludes the writer's control: clearly, Michel had 'forced himself' upon his creator. This review gave Gide particular pleasure; it turned out to be not by a man, as he had assumed, but by Loup Mayrisch, feminist, socialist, wife of a Luxembourg industrialist and a close friend of his friend Mme Théo van Rysselberghe, wife of the Belgian painter, writing under her maiden name.

Not surprisingly, the view that most accurately reflected Gide's own came from the 'frank comrade' of its dedication, Henri Ghéon, writer and practising doctor of medicine. After praising the book's classical virtues, Gide's companion on innumerable sexual adventures brushes aside any notion that Michel's homosexuality lies at the *centre* of the work. *L'Immoraliste* may be a cause of scandal, but the scandal is a general, not a 'special' one. What Michel seeks is not pleasure, of this or that kind, but the free play of instinct. The whole drama springs from a 'profound antinomy': acquired instinct is no longer instinct; it becomes a negative force, the negation of culture. When he abandons all that he has acquired in life, when he believes that he has found his true self, he is left with nothing. At once critique and apologia (and therefore solely neither), *L'Immoraliste* confronts 'the fundamental, eternal problem of the moral conditions of our existence', the gap between what we were and what we have become. Ghéon remained Gide's closest friend until the middle of the First World War, when, as Gide put it, 'God confiscated him', not in death, but in a conversion to the Catholicism of his childhood.

The Immoralist

I will praise thee; for I am fearfully and wonderfully made

Psalm 139:121

To Henri Ghéon
his frank comrade
A. G.

Preface

I present this book for what it is worth. It is a fruit filled with bitter ash, like those colocynths which sprout in the most arid deserts: rather than quench your thirst, they scorch your mouth even more, yet against their backdrop of golden sand they are not without a certain beauty.

If I had intended to set my hero up as an exemplary figure, I admit that I would have failed. Those few people who bothered to take an interest in Michel's story did so only to revile him with the full force of their rectitude. Giving Marceline so many virtues was not a waste of time: Michel was not forgiven for putting himself before her.

If I had intended this book to stand as an indictment of Michel, however, I would not have had much more success, for no one was grateful for having been made to feel so indignant towards my hero. Apparently, they felt this indignation in spite of me. This then spilled over from Michel on to me – in some people's minds, I was all but confused with him.

But I no more wanted this book to be an accusation than an apology. I refrained from passing judgement. These days the public demands an author's moral at the end of the story. In fact, they even want him to take sides as the drama unfolds, to declare himself explicitly for Alceste or for Philinte, for Hamlet or for Ophelia, for Faust or for Gretchen, for Adam or for Jehovah. It is not that I wish to claim that neutrality (I was going to say *indecision*) is a sure indicator of a superior intelligence, but I believe that many great minds have refused to . . . draw conclusions – and that posing a problem is not the same as presupposing its resolution.

I use the word 'problem' with some reluctance. In truth, in art there are no problems, none to which the work itself is not an adequate solution.

ANDRÉ GIDE

If by 'problem' we mean 'drama', I will say that the one recounted in this book, though it unfolds within the very soul of my hero, is no less universal for being circumscribed by the particularity of his experiences. I don't pretend to have invented this 'problem' – it existed before my book came along. Whether Michel prevails or not, the 'problem' continues to exist, and does not in the author's view terminate in triumph or defeat.

If certain distinguished persons have refused to see this drama as anything other than the unfolding of a particular, unusual case, and its hero as anything other than an individual with an illness, they have failed to see that there are important ideas of interest to many to be found in it. The fault does not lie with those ideas or this drama, but with the author, by which I mean his lack of skill, though he has invested all his passion, all his tears and all his care in this book. But the true interest of a work and that which any given readership might take in it are two separate things. I don't think it is too conceited to take the chance of not attracting immediate interest in matters which are inherently interesting rather than to enthuse a fickle and faddish public with no thought to the longer term.

After all, I am not trying to prove anything, merely to paint my picture well and set it in a good light.

Sidi b. M., 30 July 189–

Yes, my dear brother, Michel has spoken to us, as you thought he would. Here is the account he gave us. You asked to hear it and I promised to tell you, but at the point of sending it to you I still hesitate, the more times I reread it, the more terrible it seems. Oh, what will you think of our friend? For that matter, what do I think of him myself? . . . Shall we simply reprove his actions without admitting that such manifestly cruel faculties could be turned to good purpose? But I suspect that a fair few others would be bold enough to recognize themselves in this tale. Can we find some way of utilizing such intelligence and strength, or must we banish it from our midst?

In what way might Michel be useful to the state? I confess I don't know . . . He needs a job Could you use the high office your talents have so richly deserved, and the influence you exert, to find him something? Please hurry. Michel is a devoted person – he still is; but soon that devotion will have no other object than himself.

I write to you beneath a sky of perfect blue. In the twelve days that Denis, Daniel and I have been here, we have not seen a single cloud, nor any break in the intensity of the sun. Michel says that the sky has been crystal-clear for two months.

I am neither sad nor joyous. The air here fills you with an indefinable feeling of excitement, something which is as far from joy as it is from pain. Perhaps it is happiness.

We stay close to Michel, we don't want to leave him – you will understand why when you read these pages. It is therefore here, in his home, that we await your response. Do not delay.

You know how close Michel, Denis, Daniel and I have been since school, and how those close ties have grown even stronger over the years. The four of us have formed a sort of pact: if one of us is in need, the other three must respond to his call. So when I received Michel's mysterious cry for help, I immediately alerted the others, and we dropped everything and set off together.

We hadn't seen Michel for three years. He had got married and had gone travelling with his new wife. When he last passed through Paris, Denis was in Greece, Daniel in Russia and I, as you know, was tending our sick father. We weren't without news of him; but the reports brought by Silas and Will, who had seen him more recently, were somewhat surprising. He had changed, in ways that we were unable to explain at the time. He was no longer the bookish puritan of old, whose convictions rendered his behaviour so awkward, who could arrest our loose talk with his piercing gaze. He was . . . but I won't reveal what his own story will tell you.

Here is his story, then, just as Denis, Daniel and I heard it. Michel told it to us as we lounged on his terrace in the starlit night. When he reached the end of his story, dawn was breaking over the plain. Michel's house looks down over it and the village which is not too far away. In the heat, with its crops all gathered in, this plain looks like a desert.

Michel's house, though poor and rather odd-looking, is charming. It must get cold in the winter, as there is no glass in the windows – they aren't really windows at all, simply large holes in the walls. It is so mild we can sleep out of doors on mats.

I should also say that we had a good journey. We arrived here in the evening, exhausted by the heat, stimulated by the novelty, having stopped only briefly in Algiers and Constantine. At Constantine we caught another train to Sidi b. M., where a small cart was waiting for us. The road peters out some way short of the village, which is perched high on a rock like certain towns in Umbria. We climbed up on foot; a pair of mules carried our luggage. By this route, Michel's is the first house one comes to in the village. It is surrounded by a walled garden, or rather a paddock, in which grow three stunted pomegranate trees and a superb oleander. A Kabyle boy ran away when he saw us coming, scaling the wall with ease.

Michel made no fuss when he received us; his greetings were bland, as if he feared any display of tenderness. When we reached the threshold, however, he kissed each of us solemnly.

We barely exchanged a word until nightfall. A very frugal supper was laid out in the drawing-room, whose sumptuous decorations astonished us at the time, though they will be explained by his story. Afterwards he served us coffee, *which he insisted on preparing himself. Then we went up to the terrace, from where the view stretched away to infinity, and like the three friends of Job we waited, gazing in admiration at the plain alight with the embers of the fast-dying day.*

Once night had fallen, Michel began:

FIRST PART

I

My dear friends, I knew I could rely on your loyalty. You came running to my call as I would have done to yours. Yet we have not seen each other for three years. I hope that our friendship, which has survived this absence so well, will also survive the tale I am about to tell you. For if my call seemed an urgent one, if I made you travel so far to find me, it was purely so that I might see you, and that you might listen to me. That is all I require: the chance to speak to you. For I have reached a point in my life where I can't go on. It is not a question of weariness – I no longer understand anything. I need . . . I need to talk, as I say. Knowing how to free oneself is nothing; the difficult thing is knowing how to live with that freedom. Bear with me as I speak about myself; I am going to tell you the story of my life. I will talk plainly, with neither modesty nor pride, more plainly than if I were talking to myself. Listen to what I have to say.

The last time we all saw each other, as I recall, was on the day of my wedding in that little country church near Angers. We had invited only a small number, and having my closest friends around me turned this mundane little ceremony into something quite touching. I had the feeling that everyone found it moving – and that was what moved me. After the service we gathered at my bride's house for a light meal; there was no raucous celebration or laughter. Then we left in a hired carriage: that traditional wedding-day scene of being waved away on a journey.

I hardly knew my wife; I doubt she knew me any better. This caused me no distress. It was a loveless marriage, largely a sop to my dying father, who was worried about leaving me on my own. I loved my father dearly. Absorbed as I was in his suffering, my only thought at this sad time was to make his end easier. So I made a life commitment before I had explored the possibilities of what my life could be. There was no laughter at our engagement at my father's bedside, but there was a certain grave happiness at how much peace this brought him. I may not love my fiancée, I told myself, but at least I have never loved another woman. In my view that was enough to ensure our happiness. Still knowing myself so little, I believed I was giving myself to her totally. She was also an orphan and lived with her two brothers. She was called Marceline; she was barely twenty; I was four years older than her.

I said that I didn't love her – that is, I didn't feel for her what is normally thought of as love, but I did love her in the sense that I felt a tenderness, a sort of pity, and finally a very great respect for her. She was a Catholic, and I am a Protestant . . . yet so little of one! The priest accepted me, I accepted the priest, so everything went off smoothly.

My father was what is known as an 'atheist' – at least, I suppose he was, for, out of some deep feeling of embarrassment, which I think he shared, I had never broached the subject of his beliefs with him. The stern Huguenot upbringing given to me by my mother had, along with her cherished image, gradually faded from my mind – as you know, I was quite young when she died. I had little sense then of how the early moral lessons of childhood can exert an influence, of the traces they leave in the mind. That austerity I had inherited from my mother's indoctrination I brought to bear on my studies. I was fifteen when I lost my mother. My father took care of me, and threw himself into my education. I already had a good command of Latin and Greek; with him I quickly learned Hebrew, Sanskrit and Arabic. I was so advanced at the age of twenty that he made me his academic associate. The thought that I was his equal amused him, and he wanted to prove it to me. The *Essay on Phrygian Cults*, which appeared under his name, was my work – he scarcely even revised it, and it brought him more praise than anything he had written. He was delighted. As for me, I was somewhat taken aback at the success of this deception. But that was the start of my career. The most learned scholars treated me as their colleague. It makes me smile now to think of all the honours they bestowed on me . . . Thus I reached the age of twenty-five, having thought of little else but ruins and books, and knowing nothing about life. I poured all my energy into my work. I had a few friends (you among them), but I loved friendship more than the friends themselves – I was truly devoted to them, but out of a sense of my own nobility; I cherished all my finer feelings. After all, I knew my friends as little as I knew myself. It never occurred to me that I could lead a different life, that there was a different way to live.

My father and I had simple needs. We spent so little money that I reached the age of twenty-five not knowing that we were rich. I had always believed, not that I thought about it much, that we had just enough to live on, and I had picked up such thrifty habits from my father that I was even somewhat disturbed to find out how much we owned. I was so detached from such things at the time that even after my father's death, though I was his only heir, I was unable to form a clear idea of the scale of my fortune. This happened only when I came to be married, and realized that Marceline was bringing next to nothing to the union.

Another thing of which I was unaware, something perhaps even more important, was that my health was very fragile. How could I have known? I had never subjected it to any test. I had the occasional cold, which I ignored. The excessively quiet life I led both made me feeble and protected me from illness at the same time. Marceline, on the other hand, seemed robust – how much more so than I we were soon to discover.

On our wedding night we slept in my apartment in Paris, where two rooms had been prepared. We stayed in Paris only long enough to buy a few essential items, then travelled to Marseille, from where we embarked for Tunis.

All the things that had demanded my attention, the bewildering speed of recent events, the unavoidable emotion of the wedding following hard on the heels of the more genuine emotions of my bereavement, had all worn me out. It was only when we were on the boat that my tiredness caught up with me. Until then, all my commitments, while adding to my fatigue, had also taken my mind off it. The enforced leisure of the crossing finally gave me time to reflect. It felt to me as if it were for the very first time.

Also for the first time I had agreed to take a long break from my work. I had only ever allowed myself short holidays before then. One trip to Spain with my father, shortly after the death of my mother, had, admittedly, lasted more than a month; another, to Germany, six weeks; there had been a few others. But these were study trips; my father never allowed himself to be distracted from his painstaking research; when I wasn't accompanying him, I used to read. And yet, as soon as we left Marseille, memories of Grenada and Seville came back to me: the clearer skies, the deeper shadows, the festivals, laughter, singing. That is what we are about to experience, I thought. I went up on deck and watched Marseille recede into the distance.

Then suddenly I thought I might be neglecting Marceline.

She was sitting in the prow. I approached her and, for the first time, really looked at her.

Marceline was very pretty. You know that, you have seen her. I reproached myself for not having noticed it before. I had known her too long to see her afresh — our families had been friendly for ages, I had watched her grow up, I was used to her gracefulness . . . for the first time I was struck by how graceful she really was.

She was wearing a simple black straw hat with a large veil; she was blonde, but did not appear delicate. Her skirt and bodice were made out of the Scottish shawl we had chosen together. I didn't want her to wear the black of mourning on my account.

She sensed that I was looking at her and turned to face me . . . Until then, the attentions I had paid her had been somewhat dutiful. I had substituted for love a sort of cold gallantry, which I could see bothered her a little. Did Marceline sense at that moment that I was looking at her for the first time in a different way? She in turn looked me in the eye, then, very tenderly, she smiled at me. Without saying a word, I sat down next to her. Until now I had lived for myself, or at least according to my own devices. In getting married I hadn't thought of my wife as anything other than a companion; I hadn't thought very clearly about how my life might be changed by our union. I had only just grasped that the monologue was coming to an end.

We were alone on deck. She leaned her head in my direction, I pressed it gently to me. She raised her eyes; I kissed her on the eyelids, and suddenly felt as I did so a new sort of pity. It overcame me so violently that I couldn't hold back the tears.

'What's the matter?' Marceline asked.

We began to talk. I was charmed by her words. I had developed certain opinions about how silly women were. That evening, sitting next to her, it was I who seemed the more awkward and stupid.

So she to whom I had attached my life had a whole real life of her own! So weighty was this thought that I awoke several times that night. Several times I sat up in my bunk and saw, lying in the other bunk below, Marceline, my wife, asleep.

The next morning, the sky was splendid, the sea more or less calm. A few leisurely conversations helped us to relax with each other still further. The marriage was really beginning. On the morning of the last day of October, we disembarked at Tunis.

I had intended to spend no more than a few days there. To show you how foolish I was, I could see no attractions in this new country other than Carthage and a handful of Roman ruins: Timgad, which Octave had told me about, the mosaics of Sousse, and particularly the amphitheatre of El Djem, where I planned to hasten without delay. First I had to go to Sousse, and from there take the mail coach. I was determined not to be distracted by anything on the way.

Nevertheless, Tunis came as a great surprise. The contact with new sensations aroused parts of me that had lain dormant and, through lack of use, had retained their mysterious youthfulness. I was more astonished and bewildered than amused, but what gave me the greatest pleasure was the delight Marceline took in everything.

However, every day I grew more and more tired, but I would have been ashamed to give in to it. I was coughing and had a strangely uncomfortable feeling in my upper chest. We are heading south, I thought, the warmth will perk me up.

The Sfax mail coach leaves Sousse at eight in the evening and gets to El Djem at one in the morning. We had reserved half-compartment seats. I had expected to find an old bone-shaker; however, the seats were quite comfortable. But the cold! . . . Such was our naïve trust in the mildness of southern climes that we were lightly dressed, with nothing more than a shawl between us. No sooner had we left Sousse and the shelter of its hills than the wind began to blow. It bounded across the plain, howling, whistling, it got in through every little chink in the doors; there was no protection from it. We were both chilled to the bone when we arrived, and I was exhausted by the jolts of the coach and by a terrible cough which shook me even more. What a night! When we reached El Djem there was no inn, merely a dreadful little *bordj*. What were we to do? The coach set off. The village was asleep. In the dark, which seemed vast, we could just make out the lugubrious shape of the ruins. We heard dogs howling. We stayed in a grubby little room where two wretched beds had been set up. Marceline was shivering with the cold, but at least we were out of the wind.

The next day was dismal. We were surprised when we went out to find a completely overcast sky. The wind was still blowing, but less violently than the night before. The coach would not be passing through again until evening . . . As I have said, it was a bleak day. I explored the amphitheatre in a few minutes and found it a disappointment; it even seemed ugly to me, beneath that dull sky. Perhaps my fatigue heightened my boredom. Around midday, at a loose end, I revisited it, searching in vain for inscriptions in the stones. Marceline sat out of the wind, reading an English book she had fortunately brought with her. I sat down next to her.

'What a dreary day. I hope you're not too bored.'

'No, as you see, I have something to read.'

'Why on earth did we come here? I hope you aren't feeling cold.'

'Not too cold. What about you? You're quite pale.'

'No . . .'

That night, the wind picked up again. Finally the coach arrived. We set off.

The first jolts of the coach went right through me. Marceline, who was very tired, went straight to sleep on my shoulder. My coughing will wake her, I thought, and gently, very gently disengaging myself, I propped her against the side of the coach. However, I wasn't coughing now, I was spitting. This was new. There was no strain, it came in little jerks at regular intervals. It was such a curious sensation that at first I found it almost funny, but I was soon nauseated by the strange taste it left in my mouth. My handkerchief was quickly used up. My fingers were already covered with it. Should I wake Marceline? . . . Luckily I remembered a large handkerchief she wore tucked into her belt. I removed it gently. I no longer held back and the spitting came on more strongly than before. I felt extraordinarily relieved. It's the last throes of my cold, I thought. Suddenly I felt very weak. Everything began to spin before my eyes and I thought I was going to pass out. Should I wake her? . . . The shame of it! (My puritanical childhood had, I believe, left me with this contempt for any surrender to weakness – to my mind it was cowardice.) I got a grip on myself, held on and finally overcame my dizziness . . . I imagined I was back at sea, and the sound of the wheels was the sound of the waves . . . But I had stopped spitting.

Then I drifted into a kind of sleep.

When I awoke, dawn was already breaking across the sky. Marceline was still asleep. We were almost there. The handkerchief I held in my hand was dark-coloured, so I didn't notice at first; but when I took my own handkerchief out of my pocket I was amazed to see it was covered with blood.

My first instinct was to hide the blood from Marceline. But how? I had bloodstains all over me. It was everywhere, especially on my fingers . . . I must have had a nosebleed – that's it, if she asks, I had a nosebleed.

Marceline was still sleeping. We arrived. She had to get off first, and she didn't see anything. We had two rooms reserved. I was able to dash into mine and wash the blood away. Marceline had seen nothing.

However, I felt very weak, and I ordered up some tea for both of us. And as she was pouring it, looking a little pale herself, smiling, I suddenly felt irritated that she hadn't seen anything. I knew I was being unfair. I told myself: the reason she didn't see anything was that you hid it from her. But it was no good, the feeling grew in me instinctively, and began to take hold . . . Finally it was too strong, I couldn't resist it. Casually, I remarked:

'I spat up some blood during the night.'

She didn't make a sound. She just went very pale, tottered on her feet, tried to steady herself and then collapsed heavily to the floor. I rushed to her in a sort of rage: 'Marceline! Marceline!' Hell, what have

I done? Wasn't it enough that *one of us* was ill? But, as I have said, I was very weak. I almost felt like fainting myself. I opened the door and called for help. Someone came.

In my bag I had a letter of introduction to an officer in the town. On the strength of this I sent for the army doctor.

Meanwhile, Marceline had come round and was at my bedside, where I lay shivering with fever. The doctor arrived and examined us both. Marceline was fine, he said, and had suffered no ill effects from her fall. I was seriously ill – he even refused a diagnosis, but promised to return later in the day.

When he came back he was smiling and talkative and he gave me various remedies. I realized he thought there was no hope. Dare I tell you I was barely perturbed by this? I was very tired, I simply gave up. 'After all, what is there to live for? I have worked hard to the end, done my duty with passion and dedication. Apart from that . . . oh, what else is there?' I thought, admiring my own stoicism. What was really painful was the ugliness of my surroundings. 'This room is dreadful,' I thought, looking around. Suddenly, I realized that in a similar room next to this one was my wife, Marceline. I could hear her voice. The doctor hadn't yet gone, he was talking to her, trying to keep his voice down. Then some time elapsed – I must have gone to sleep . . .

When I woke up, Marceline was there. I realized she had been crying. I didn't love life enough to feel sorry for myself, but the ugliness of this place distressed me. My eyes feasted on her.

She was sitting near by, writing. I thought she looked pretty. I saw her seal a number of letters. Then she got up, came over to the bed and took my hand tenderly:

'How are you feeling now?' she asked.

I smiled and asked sadly, 'Will I get better?'

'Of course you will,' she replied with such heartfelt conviction that I was almost convinced myself, and I had a confused intimation of what life could be, of her love, a vague but moving vision of her inner beauty. My eyes filled with tears and I wept long and hard, unable, and unwilling, to stop.

With the strength of her love, she made me leave Sousse. With tender care she took care of me, aided me, nursed me . . . From Sousse to Tunis, then from Tunis to Constantine, Marceline was magnificent. I would get better in Biskra. Her confidence was unswerving, her optimism did not waver in the slightest. She made all the arrangements, organized the journeys and booked the accommodation. Unfortunately it was beyond her power to make the journey less horrible. At several points I felt I would have to stop and give up. I was sweating like someone in his death throes, I couldn't breathe, every now and again I lost consciousness. At the end of the third day I arrived at Biskra, more dead than alive.

II

Why speak of those early days? What remains of them? Their terrible memory has no voice. I didn't know who I was or where I was. All I can recall now is the sight of Marceline, my wife, my life, leaning over my bed as I lay in agony. I am sure it was her passionate care, her love alone, that saved me. One day, finally, like a lost sailor spotting land, I felt the first glimmer of newly awakening life. I was able to smile at Marceline. Why tell you all of this? Suffice it to say that death, as the saying goes, had brushed me with its wing, that simply being alive was astonishing, that each new day was a day I had never hoped to see. Before, I thought, I had no sense that I was alive. Now the thrill of discovering life afresh.

The day came when I was able to get up. I was utterly enchanted by our home. It was little more than a terrace – but what a terrace! Both my and Marceline's rooms opened out on to it. It spread out across the rooftops. From the highest part one could see palm trees above the houses, and above the palm trees, the desert. The other side of the terrace adjoined the park; it was shaded by the branches of the nearest cassias. And it ran the length of the courtyard – a small, regular courtyard planted with six palms – ending in the staircase that connected it to the courtyard. My room was large and airy, with bare, whitewashed walls, a small door leading to Marceline's room and a French window opening on to the terrace.

There the hourless days slipped by. How many times during my solitude have I recalled those slow days! . . . Marceline next to me, reading, writing; me doing nothing, watching her. Oh, Marceline! . . . I watch: I see the sun, I see the shade, I see the edge of the shadow move. I have so little to think about that I observe it. I am still very weak, my breathing is laboured, everything tires me out, even reading. But what would I read? Simply existing is enough for me.

One morning Marceline comes in laughing:

'I've brought a friend to see you,' she says, and I see a small, dark-skinned Arab come in behind her. His name is Bachir and he looks at me with his large, silent eyes. I feel a little perturbed, and this in itself is enough to tire me. I don't say anything, I just look cross. The boy is disconcerted by this frosty welcome and turns to Marceline; like a graceful animal he nuzzles up to her cajolingly, takes her hand and embraces her, revealing his bare arms in the process. I notice that he is completely naked beneath his thin white *gandourah* and patchwork burnous.

'Go on, sit down,' Marceline says, noticing my embarrassment. 'Amuse yourself quietly.'

The boy sits down on the floor, takes a knife and a piece of *djerid* wood out of the hood of his burnous and starts to whittle away. I think he is trying to carve a whistle.

Very soon I am no longer uncomfortable in his presence. I look at him; he seems to have forgotten where he is. His feet are bare, he has the most charming ankles and wrists. The dexterity with which he wields his blunt knife is quite amusing . . . Do I really find all this interesting? . . . His hair is close-cropped in the Arab fashion. He wears a shabby *chechia* on his head, with a hole where the tassel used to be. The *gandourah* has slipped a little, revealing his dainty little shoulder. I really want to touch it. I lean over; he turns to me and smiles. I gesture to him to give me his whistle; I take it and pretend to admire it greatly. Now he wants to leave. Marceline gives him a cake, I give him two sous.

The next day, for the first time, I am bored. I am waiting for something – for what? – I feel at a loose end, restless. Finally, I can't hold out any longer:

'Isn't Bachir coming this morning?'

'If you like, I'll go and fetch him.'

She leaves me and goes out. After a while she returns, alone. What has this illness done to me? I feel like crying when I see her come back without Bachir.

'I was too late,' she says. 'School had finished and the children had gone home. Some of them are quite charming, you know. I think they all know me now.'

'Well, maybe you can get him to come tomorrow.'

The next day Bachir returned. He sat down as he had the day before, took out his knife and tried to whittle some wood that was too hard. In the end the blade skidded into his thumb. I shuddered with horror, but he just laughed it off, showing off the glistening cut and watching the flow of blood with an air of amusement. When he laughed, he showed his pure white teeth. He licked the cut blithely; his tongue was pink like a cat's. Ah, how well he looked. That is what I fell in love with – his health. This small body was in beautiful health.

The following day he brought some marbles. He wanted me to play with him. Marceline wasn't there – she would have stopped me. I hesitated, I looked at Bachir. He grabbed my arm, placed the marbles in my hand, egged me on. The effort of bending down left me short of breath, but I tried to play anyway. Finally, I couldn't manage it any more. I was streaming with sweat. I threw the marbles down and fell back into a chair. Bachir looked at me, somewhat concerned.

'Sick?' he said softly. The timbre of his voice was exquisite. Marceline came back in.

'Take him away,' I said. 'I'm tired this morning.'

A few hours later I spat up some blood. It was while I was attempting to take a walk on the terrace. Marceline was busy in her room, luckily she didn't see any of this. Feeling a bit breathless, I had inhaled more deeply than usual, and suddenly it came. It filled my mouth . . . But it wasn't clear blood like the first time, it was a horrible, thick clot which I spat on the ground in disgust.

I took a few steps and tottered. I was shaken by it, I was trembling. I was afraid, I was angry, for until now I had thought that the cure was slowly taking its course, and I only needed to be patient. I had had a cruel setback. The strange thing is that the first time the spitting had come I wasn't too affected; I seemed to recall I was quite calm. So what was the reason for my present fear and dread? Alas, it was because I had started to love life.

I came back, bent over, found the clot, picked it up with a piece of straw and placed it in my handkerchief. I looked at it. It was a nasty dark colour, almost black, sticky and horrible . . . I thought of Bachir's beautiful, glistening blood . . . And suddenly I felt a wish, a desire, more pressing and imperious than anything I had ever felt before, to live! I want to live. I want to live. I clenched my teeth, my fists, concentrated my whole being into this wild, desperate drive towards existence.

The day before, I had received a letter from T—; in response to Marceline's anxious inquiries it was full of medical advice. He had even enclosed a few popular medical pamphlets and a more specialized book, which I took more seriously. I had idly skimmed the letter and not consulted the publications at all, first because their resemblance to those little moral tracts I was force-fed as a child did not dispose me in their favour, and also because I found all advice irksome. Besides, I didn't think that *Advice to Tuberculosis Sufferers* or *A Practical Cure for Tuberculosis* really applied to my case. I didn't believe I had tuberculosis. I preferred to attribute my first haemorrhage to a different cause. To tell the truth, I didn't attribute it to anything at all, I avoided having to think about it, did not, in fact, think about it much, and considered myself, if not cured, then at least well on the road to recovery . . . I read the letter, I devoured the book and the pamphlets. Suddenly it became frighteningly obvious that I had not been looking after myself as I should. Until then I had been drifting along, trusting in the vaguest of hopes. Suddenly I saw my life under attack, vilely assaulted at its very heart. An active enemy was living and breeding inside me. I could hear it, observe it, feel it. I wouldn't beat it without a fight . . . and I added out loud, as if to convince myself more fully: it's a question of willpower.

I placed myself on a war footing.

Dusk was falling. I planned my strategy. For the time being, my studies would concentrate solely on my cure, my only duty was to my health. I would identify as *good* only those things that were salutary to me, forget, reject anything that did not contribute to my cure. By supper-time I had made resolutions concerning breathing, exercise and diet.

We took our meals in a sort of little kiosk surrounded on each side by the terrace. Alone, peaceful, far from everything, we enjoyed the intimacy of these meals. An old negro brought us passable food from a neighbouring hotel. Marceline supervised the menus, ordered such and such a dish, rejected another . . . Given my general lack of appetite, I didn't care too much if the meals weren't up to scratch, or the menus were insufficient. Marceline, herself no big eater, didn't realize that I wasn't eating enough. To eat more was the first of my resolutions. I intended to put it into effect that very evening. I couldn't: we had some totally inedible salami, followed by a ridiculously overdone roast.

I was so annoyed that I took it out on Marceline. I vented my spleen in a stream of intemperate language. I blamed her. To listen to me, it was as if I were holding her responsible for the poor quality of the food. This small delay in the start of the diet I had resolved to adopt became a matter of the utmost importance. I forgot about the preceding days; this one ruined meal spoiled everything. I put my foot down. Marceline was forced to go down into the town to find a tin or jar of something.

She came straight back with a small terrine, which I devoured almost in its entirety, as if to prove to both of us how much I needed to eat more.

That same evening we agreed on the following: the meals would be significantly better and more frequent – one every three hours, the first at half past six. A plentiful supply of varied tinned food would supplement the mediocre fare of the hotel . . .

I couldn't sleep that night, so stimulated was I by the thought of my new-found virtues. I think I had a touch of fever. I had a bottle of mineral water by the bed. I drank a glass, then another; on the third occasion, I drank straight from the bottle, emptying it in one go. I went over my new resolve in my head, as if learning a lesson: I honed my hostility, directed it at all and sundry. I had to fight against everything: my salvation depended on myself.

Finally, I saw the sky lighten; the day dawned.

It had been my vigil before the battle.

The next day was Sunday. I must confess that, prior to this, I had taken no interest in Marceline's religious beliefs. Whether out of indifference or embarrassment, I had thought that it was none of my business; besides, I didn't attach any importance to the matter. That day Marceline went to mass. I learned when she came back that she had prayed for me. I looked her in the eye, then, as gently as I could, said:

'There's no need to pray for me, Marceline.'

'Why not?' she asked, a little troubled.

'I don't like special favours.'

'You would reject God's help?'

'I would have to be grateful to him. It creates obligations, and I don't want any.'

Though we made light of it, neither of us was in any doubt about the seriousness of what we said.

'You won't get better on your own, my poor darling,' she sighed.

'Then so be it . . .' Then, noticing her sad expression, I added, less abruptly, 'You will help me.'

III

I am going to talk at some length about my body. I am going to talk about it so much that you will think at first that I am neglecting the mind entirely. The omission is quite intentional; it is how it was. I don't have the strength to lead a dual life, I said to myself. I'll think about the life of the mind later, when I am feeling better.

I was still far from feeling well. The slightest thing put me into a sweat, or gave me a chill. I suffered from a 'shortness of breath', as Rousseau put it; I was sometimes feverish. Often in the morning I felt a terrible weariness and I lay slumped in an armchair, interested in nothing, self-absorbed, concentrating solely on the act of breathing. I breathed with difficulty, methodically, carefully. My breath came out in two short gasps, which my heightened willpower could only partially control. Even long afterwards, I could only prevent this if I really paid attention.

But the thing I suffered from most was my susceptibility to the smallest changes of temperature. Looking back, I think my illness was compounded by some nervous disorder. I can't think of any other explanation for a series of symptoms which couldn't be attributed merely to the tuberculosis. I was always either too hot or too cold. I would put on a ridiculous number of layers, then only stop shivering when I started sweating; when I took some layers off, I would start shivering when the sweating stopped. Parts of my body would be freezing – in spite of the sweat, they would feel as cold as marble; I could do nothing to warm them up. I was so sensitive to the cold that even splashing a drop of water on my foot as I washed would give me a chill. It was the same with heat . . . I never lost this sensitivity, I still have it now, but these days it is a source of exquisite pleasure. I believe that any heightened sensitivity can be a source of pleasure or pain, depending on the strength or weakness of one's constitution. Everything that was painful to me then is now a delight.

I don't know how I had managed until then to sleep with the windows closed. On T—'s advice I tried to open them at night – a little at first, then before long I had them wide open. Soon it became a habit, a need so great that whenever the windows were closed I felt stifled. And later, how delicious that feeling of the night breeze, the moonlight.

But enough of these first splutterings of health. Thanks to careful nursing, the clean air, the best food, I soon began to pick up. Before, my breathlessness put me off tackling the steps, and I didn't dare leave the terrace. Towards the end of January, however, I ventured down into the park.

Marceline came with me, carrying a shawl. It was three o'clock in the afternoon. The wind, which is often strong in these parts, and which had been giving me a lot of discomfort in the previous three days, had dropped. The air was delightfully mild.

The town park . . . It is bisected by a wide path canopied by two rows of those very tall mimosas known round here as cassias. In the shade of these trees there are benches. A channelled stream – by which I mean it is deeper than it is wide – flows alongside the path in a more or less straight line. Then there are smaller channels, distributing the water from the stream to the plants in the other parts of the gardens. The water is thick and muddy, pinkish-grey like the clay. Hardly any foreigners, just a few Arabs; as they walk out of the sun, their white cloaks take on the colour of the shadows.

I felt an odd shiver come over me as I walked into this strange shade. I wrapped myself in my shawl. Yet I didn't feel unwell, quite the opposite . . . We sat down on a bench. Marceline was quiet. Some Arabs walked past, then a group of children. Marceline knew quite a few of them and waved. They came over. She told me their names. They exchanged questions and answers, smiled, pouted, played little games. This bothered me somewhat, and I could feel my unease returning. I was tired and perspiring. But to be honest, what really made me feel uncomfortable was not the children, it was her. Yes, however little, she was in the way. If I had got up, she would have followed me; if I had taken off my shawl, she would have offered to carry it; if I had put it straight back on, she would have asked, 'Are you cold?' And I wouldn't dare speak to the children in front of her – I could see she had her favourites. In spite of myself, but none the less deliberately, I showed more interest in the others.

'Let's go,' I said, and I decided I would come back to the park on my own.

The next day she had to go out around ten o'clock. I made the most of it. Little Bachir, who rarely missed a morning, carried my shawl. I felt alert, light of heart. We were virtually alone on the path. I walked slowly, taking breaks to sit down. Bachir walked behind me, chattering away, as faithful and docile as a dog. I reached the part of the canal where the washerwomen did their work. There is a flat stone in the middle of the stream, and on it lay a girl, face downwards, trailing her hand in the water, throwing and catching twigs. She had been paddling in the stream; her feet were still damp, making the skin look darker. Bachir went up to her and spoke to her. She turned round, gave me a smile and replied to Bachir in Arabic.

'She's my sister,' he said. Then he explained that their mother was coming to do her laundry, and his little sister was waiting for her. She was called Rhadra, which is Arabic for 'green'. He said all this in a voice that was as charming, pure and child-like as the emotion it aroused in me.

'She wants you to give her two sous,' he said.

I gave her ten and was getting ready to set off when her mother, the washerwoman, turned up. She was a handsome, well-built woman, with a wide forehead covered in blue tattoos. She carried a linen basket on her head like a Greek caryatid; like a caryatid too, she was draped in a single piece of dark blue cloth, which was tied at the waist and fell to her feet. When she saw Bachir she shouted something at him. He replied angrily, the little girl joined in, and soon all three were involved in a heated discussion. Finally, Bachir admitted defeat and came to tell me that his mother needed him that morning. He handed back my shawl sadly and I had to go on alone.

I had taken barely twenty steps when the weight of the shawl became unbearable. Bathed in sweat, I sat down on the first bench I could find. I hoped some child would come along who could relieve me of my burden. The boy who did come along was a tall fourteen-year-old, dark as a Sudanese, not shy in the slightest, and he offered to help of his own accord. He was called Ashour. I would have found him handsome were he not blind in one eye. He loved to talk; he told me where the stream came from, and that when it left the park it flowed right through the oasis. I listened to him and forgot my fatigue. For all that I liked Bachir, I knew him too well now and I was glad to have a change. I even promised myself I would come to the park on my own one day, sit on a bench and wait for some pleasant chance encounter . . .

After several stops along the way, Ashour and I arrived at my front door. I wanted to ask him up, but I didn't dare, as I didn't know how Marceline would react.

I found her in the dining-room, tending a small boy who looked so sickly and wretched that I felt more disgust than pity.

Somewhat fearfully, Marceline said, 'The poor boy is ill.'

'I hope it's not contagious. What's wrong with him?'

'I'm not sure exactly. He seems to be hurting all over. His French is very bad. When Bachir comes tomorrow, he'll have to interpret for us . . . I'm making him drink a little tea . . .' Then, as if to explain herself, and because I was standing there not saying a word, she added, 'I've known him a long time. I haven't had the nerve to bring him here before. I was afraid of tiring you, or displeasing you.'

'Why should it?' I shouted. 'Bring all the children you like, if it amuses you!' And it was with some irritation that I realized I could have brought Ashour up after all.

Yet I looked at my wife. She was so maternal with her caresses. Her tenderness was so touching that the boy looked quite restored when he left. I told her about my walk and gently explained to her why I'd rather go out alone.

At that time I was still waking up most nights either frozen or bathed in sweat. That night I slept virtually undisturbed. The next morning I was ready to go out by nine o'clock. It was a fine day, I felt well rested, not at all weak. I was happy, or rather in high spirits. The air was calm and warm, but I took my shawl anyway, so that I might ask someone

ANDRÉ GIDE

to carry it and thereby strike up an acquaintance. I have mentioned
that the park adjoins our terrace, so I got there in no time. I walked
into its shade with a sense of rapture. The air was luminous. The cassias,
which flower long before they come into leaf, gave off a sweet scent –
or perhaps it emanated from everywhere, that light, unfamiliar smell
which seemed to enter into me by all my senses and filled me with a
feeling of exaltation. I was breathing more easily, walking with a lighter
step. I did have to sit down on the first bench, but I was more intoxicated,
more dazzled than tired. I looked around. The shadows were light and
fleeting; they didn't fall on the ground, they barely skimmed it. O light!
I listened. What could I hear? Nothing, everything; every sound amused
me. I remember a shrub whose bark, from a distance, seemed to have
such a strange texture that I had to get up to go over and feel it. My
touch was a caress, it filled me with rapture. I remember . . . was this
finally the morning when I was to be born?

I had forgotten I was alone; I sat there, waiting for nothing, oblivious
to the time. Until that day, it seemed to me, I had felt so little and
thought so much, and I was astonished to find that my sensations were
becoming as strong as thoughts. I say 'it seemed to me', for from the
depths of my early childhood the glimmer of a myriad lost sensations
was re-emerging. With my new-found awareness of my own senses I
was able to recognize them, albeit tentatively. Yes, as my senses awoke,
they rediscovered a whole history, reconstructed a whole past life. They
were alive! Alive! They had never ceased to live but throughout my
years of study had led a secret, latent existence.

I met no one that day, and I was glad of it. I took out of my pocket
a small edition of Homer which I hadn't opened since I had left
Marseille, reread three lines of the *Odyssey*, learned them by heart,
then, finding enough to nourish me in their rhythm, savoured them at
my leisure. I shut the book and sat there trembling, more alive than I
thought possible, my spirit drowsy with happiness . . .

IV

Meanwhile, Marceline, noting with delight that I was finally coming back to health, began to talk about the wonderful orchards of the oasis. She loved the open air. My illness had given her enough free time to go off on long walks, from which she returned full of enthusiasm. Previously she had hardly mentioned them, in case I got the urge to go with her and had to face the disappointment of hearing about pleasures in which I could not yet indulge myself. But now that I was getting better, she thought the enticement might help to advance my recovery. I was buoyed up by my new-found love of walking and exploring. The very next day we went out together.

She walked ahead of me on a path so strange I had never seen the like in any other country. It weaves its way lazily between two fairly high earth walls, twisting and turning around the gardens which the walls enclose; in places it bends, in others it breaks off entirely; no sooner are you on it than you strike off at a tangent; you soon lose track of where you have come from or where you are going. The faithful old stream follows the line of the path, skirting the walls on one side. The walls themselves are made of the same earth as the path, and the oasis as a whole, a delicate pinkish-grey clay; this takes on a darker hue in the water, cracks in the sun, hardens in the heat, but softens again with the first spot of rain, becoming a pliable loam which retains the imprint of every bare footstep. Palm trees rise above the walls. Turtle-doves flew out of them as we approached. Marceline looked at me.

I forgot about my tiredness and discomfort. I walked along in a state of ecstasy, a sort of silent joy, an exaltation of the senses and the flesh.

Suddenly there was a light gust of wind; all the palms shook and we saw the taller ones bend over. Then the air became quite calm again and I could distinctly hear the sound of a flute coming from behind a wall. We found a gap and went through.

The place was full of light and shadow, tranquil, as if outside time, full of silence and quivering with the gentle trickling of the water flowing from tree to tree, irrigating the palms, the soft cooing of the doves, the sound of a child playing the flute. He was tending a herd of goats. He was sitting, virtually naked, on the trunk of a fallen palm tree. He wasn't concerned by our presence, he didn't run away; he interrupted his playing only for a moment.

During this quiet interlude I realized that there was another flute answering from afar. We carried on a little further, then Marceline said, 'There's no point in going on; these orchards all look the same, except perhaps at the other end of the oasis they are slightly bigger . . .' She spread the shawl on the ground. 'Take a rest.'

How long did we stay there? I have no idea. What does time matter? Marceline was by my side. I lay down and rested my head on her knees. The sound of the flute still flowed, breaking off occasionally, then starting again. The sound of the water . . . The odd bleat of a goat. I closed my eyes. I felt Marceline's cool hand rest on my forehead. I felt the hot sun gently filtered by the palms. My mind was blank – what was the point of thinking? I felt extra-ordinarily . . .

Then at odd moments, a new sound. I opened my eyes, it was the breeze in the palms; it didn't reach us down below, it merely stirred the highest branches . . .

The next morning I went back to this same garden with Marceline. In the afternoon of that same day, I went on my own. The goatherd was there with his flute. I went up and spoke to him. He was called Lassif, he was only twelve and he was very handsome. He told me the canals were called *seghias*. They weren't full of water every day, apparently. The water is rationed prudently – when it has quenched the thirst of a given tree it is closed off. Each palm has a small trough hollowed out at its base to hold just enough to water the tree. The boy demonstrated how an ingenious system of sluices controls the water and directs it to where the need is greatest.

The following day I saw one of Lassif's brothers. He was a little older, but less handsome; his name was Lachmi. He climbed to the top of a pollarded palm using the stumps of sawn-off branches as a makeshift ladder; then he descended agilely, his cloak billowing to reveal his naked golden flesh. He brought down a small earthenware gourd which had been hanging from the severed tip of the tree gathering the sap which is used to make a sweet wine to which the Arabs are very partial. At Lachmi's prompting I tried some, but I didn't like the insipid, sour, syrupy taste.

The following days I went further. I saw other gardens, other orchards and other goats. As Marceline had said, these gardens were all the same; yet each one was subtly different.

Sometimes Marceline still came with me, but more often, once we reached the orchards, I left her, convincing her that I was tired and needed to sit down, that there was no need for her to stay with me, that she needed the exercise, so that she would go on without me. I stayed with the children. Soon I got to know quite a few of them. I had long conversations with them, learned their games, taught them others, lost all my loose change at pitch and toss. Some of them came with me on my walks (every day I went further) and showed me new routes back, looked after my cloak and shawl on the occasions I brought both. Before leaving them I handed out some loose change. Sometimes they followed me, still playing, to my door. Finally, I got them to come inside.

Marceline also brought some children home with her. They came from school, and she encouraged them to do their homework. It was the good children and the shy ones who came after school. The ones I brought were different, but they all joined in the games together. We made sure we always had syrups and sweets to hand. Soon more came, without even being invited by us. I can remember every one of them, I can see them now . . .

Towards the end of January, the weather took a sharp turn for the worse. A cold wind began to blow and I could feel the effects on my health immediately. The large stretch of open ground between the town and the oasis became uncrossable, and I had to content myself once more with the park. Then it began to rain, an icy rain that blanketed the mountains on the northern horizon with snow.

I passed mournful days by the fire, struggling furiously with the illness, which had gained the upper hand in this bad weather. These were depressing days; I could neither read nor work; the slightest effort brought me out in an uncomfortable sweat; trying to concentrate exhausted me; when I stopped paying attention to my breathing, I began to suffocate.

During these dreary days the children were my only distraction. When it was raining, only the ones we knew best came to visit. Their clothes were drenched; they would sit in a circle round the fire. There were long gaps when no one said a word. I was too tired, in too much pain to do anything other than look at them. But seeing their good health made me feel better. Marceline's favourites were too weak and sickly, and too well-behaved. I was irritated by both her and them, and in the end I kept them at a distance. To tell the truth, they frightened me.

One morning, I had a strange moment of self-revelation. Moktir, the only one of my wife's favourites who didn't annoy me (perhaps because he was good-looking), was alone with me in my room. Until then I had liked him only moderately, but his dark, brilliant eyes intrigued me. I developed an inexplicable curiosity about him, and began to watch his movements carefully. I was standing by the fire, my elbows resting on the mantelpiece, apparently absorbed in my book, but I could see what the child was doing behind me by looking in the mirror. Moktir didn't realize he was being observed, he thought I was immersed in my reading. I saw him silently approach a table, pick up a pair of scissors that Marceline had left lying next to her sewing and slide them quickly inside his *burnous*. I could feel my heart pounding for a moment, but for the life of me I couldn't summon up a squeak of protest. In fact, I would have to say that the feeling that swept over me was nothing other than joy! Once I had allowed Moktir enough time to complete his theft, I turned round and spoke to him as if nothing had happened. Marceline was very fond of this child, but in retrospect

I don't think it was the fear of upsetting her that made me invent some story or other to explain the loss of her scissors, rather than denounce Moktir. From that day on, Moktir became my favourite.

V

Our stay at Biskra was coming to an end. Once the February rains had passed, the hot weather suddenly descended. After several dreary days of incessant downpour, I awoke one morning to a sky of brilliant blue. As soon as I got up, I hurried to the upper terrace. There was not a cloud in the sky as far as the eye could see. Billows of mist were rising in the sun, which was already burning hot; the whole oasis was steaming. In the distance I could hear the rush of the Oued in flood. The air was so pure and fresh I felt better immediately. Marceline came up; we wanted to go out, but on that particular day it was too muddy.

A few days later we went back to Lassif's orchard. The stems of the plants looked heavy, soft, swollen with water. After its long period of waiting, of which I had no knowledge, after days of being submerged by the rains, this African earth was now awakening from winter, drunk with water, bursting with new sap. It rejoiced in a frenzy of spring, striking an echo in my own feelings. Ashour and Moktir came with us at first. I still enjoyed their easy friendship, and it cost me only half a franc a day. But soon I tired of them: I was no longer so weak that I needed the spectacle of their health, and their games no longer fed my happiness in the way I needed. I directed the exaltation of my mind and senses towards Marceline. Seeing the joy this gave her, I realized that before she must have been sad. I apologized like a child for having neglected her so often, attributed my strange moodiness to my illness, and promised that, whereas until now I had been too weary to love, henceforth my love would grow with my health. I meant it, but I must have still been very weak, for it was over a month later that I first began to feel desire for Marceline.

The heat, however, grew more intense by the day. There was nothing now to keep us in Biskra – except its charm, which would draw me back there at a later date. We made a sudden decision to leave. We were packed within three hours. The train left the next day at dawn . . .

I remember our last night. The moon was almost full, its light poured into my room through my wide-open window. Marceline was asleep, I think. I was in bed, but couldn't sleep. I was burning with a sort of fever of happiness, which was nothing other than life itself . . . I got up, bathed my hands and face in water, then opened the French window and went out.

It was already late. There wasn't a sound, not a breath of wind; it was as if the air had gone to sleep. I could only just hear, in the distance, the Arab dogs, which yap all night like jackals. Before me was the small courtyard, bisected by the slanting shadow of the facing wall. The regularly spaced palm trees, drained of their colour and life, looked as if they would never stir again . . . But in sleep there is still the beat of life. Here nothing seemed to be sleeping, everything seemed dead. This quietness frightened me, and once again all my negative feelings about my life came back, protesting, asserting their presence, bewailing their existence in the silence. They were so violent, painful almost, so insistent that, if I could, I would have howled like an animal. I took hold of my hand, I recall, took my left hand in my right; I wanted to raise it to my head, and did so. Why? To confirm that I was still alive and to show myself how wonderful that was. I touched my forehead, my eyelids. I was seized by a shudder. One day, I thought, one day I will not even have the strength to raise water to my lips when I am dying of thirst . . . I went back in, but did not go straight to bed. I wanted to fix the memory of this night in my mind, so as not to lose it. Not knowing what else to do, I picked up a book from the table – the Bible – and opened it at random. I could read by the light of the moon. I read Christ's words to Peter, words, alas, which I was never to forget: 'When you were young, you girded yourself and walked where you would; but when you are old, you will stretch out your hands . . .' You will stretch out your hands . . .

The next day, we left at dawn.

41

VI

I won't tell you about the journey in detail. Some parts of it I can only remember vaguely. My health still fluctuated; I would falter when a cold wind picked up, grow anxious when a passing cloud cast its shadow, and my nerves were a constant source of trouble. But at least my lungs were recovering. Each relapse was shorter and less serious: the assault was as fierce, but my body's defences were better able to cope.

From Tunis we sailed to Malta, then to Syracuse. I was back in that classical land whose language and history I knew so well. Since I had fallen ill my life had been free of rules or moral scrutiny; I had merely concentrated on living, like an animal or a child. Now that I was less preoccupied with the state of my health, I was regaining awareness of the world around me and starting to determine my own life once again. After my long period of suffering, I had believed that I had been reborn intact and that my past and present formed a seamless unity. When I had had the novelty of a new country to absorb, I was thus able to deceive myself, but not here. I was constantly reminded – much to my surprise – that I had changed.

When, in Syracuse and later, I tried to take up my studies again, to immerse myself as before in the minutiae of historical research, I found that something had, if not extinguished, then in some way tempered my enthusiasm. It was my feeling for the present. For me history now had that same static quality that had terrified me in the night-time shadows of the little courtyard in Biskra: the immobility of death. Before, it had been this very fixity that I liked; it allowed my mind to work with precision. The facts of history now seemed to me like museum pieces, or rather like plants in a herbarium, so completely dried out that I could forget that they had ever grown in the sun, plump with sap. Now I could only derive pleasure from history by imagining it in the present. I was much less inspired by great political events than by the new emotions stirred by the poets or certain men of action. In Syracuse I reread Theocritus and imagined that his goatherds with their beautiful names were the same as those I had loved in Biskra.

As my erudition progressively revived it began to weigh me down and hinder my happiness. I was unable to see a Greek theatre or temple without reconstructing it in my mind. I grieved at the death of all these ancient festivals, which had left nothing but ruins in their place. I hated death.

I started to avoid ruins. The finest monuments of antiquity meant less to me than the sunken gardens of the Latomies, where the lemons have the sharp sweetness of oranges, or the banks of the Cyane, still as blue now as it flows through the papyrus as on the day it wept for Persephone.

I started to despise the learning that I used to pride myself on. My studies, which used to be my whole life, now seemed to have no more than an accidental, inessential relation to it. I had discovered that I was different and that I existed – what joy! – independently of them. As an academic, I felt foolish; as a man – did I know myself? I had only just been born and couldn't yet know who I was. This is what I had to find out.

There is nothing more tragic, for someone who has faced death, than a long convalescence. After my brush with the wing of death, the things that seemed important before no longer mattered; other things had taken their place, things which had never seemed important before, which I didn't even know existed. The accreted layers of acquired learning flaked away like greasepaint, offering glimpses of bare flesh, the real person hidden underneath.

From now on, *he* was the one I intended to discover: the authentic being, the 'old Adam' rejected by the Gospel, the one that everything in my life – books, teachers, parents, I myself – had tried to suppress. I was starting to glimpse him already, still vague and elusive, due to the accumulate layers of disguise, but all the more worthy of discovery for that. I now despised this secondary being which education had inscribed upon him. I had to shake off these layers.

I likened myself to a palimpsest. I felt the joy of a scholar who discovers, beneath newer writings, a more ancient and infinitely more precious text inscribed on the same piece of paper. What was this secret writing? Was it not necessary to efface the more recent writing in order to read it?

Besides, I was no longer the pale, scholarly creature to which my former morality, with its rigid restrictions, was so well suited. My convalescence had been more than that: I had experienced an amplification, a recrudescence of life, a pulse of richer, warmer blood which reached my thoughts, touching them one by one, penetrating everywhere, stirring and colouring the most remote, delicate and secret fibres of my being. For one adapts to one's relative strength or weakness; one's being forms itself according to the powers it possesses. But if these increase, if they allow one to do more, then . . . I wasn't thinking these things at the time, I am giving you a false picture. In truth, I didn't think at all, I didn't analyse myself in this way. I was guided by a happy sense of fatalism. I was afraid that too hasty a scrutiny would disturb the mystery of my slow transformation. One has to give the secret writing time to appear and not seek to fill it in oneself. Therefore, not so much neglecting my mind as leaving it to lie fallow, I gave myself over to the voluptuous enjoyment of myself and of everything that seemed to me divine. We had left Syracuse and I was running along the steep road between Taormina and Mola shouting, as if to summon him up within me, 'A new self! A new self!'

My only effort – and it was a constant effort – was systematically to revile or repress everything that I thought I owed to my past education and my former morality. With a determined disdain for my learning and a contempt for my scholarly ways, I refused to visit Agrigentum, and a few days later I didn't stop on the road to Naples at the fine temple of Paestum, where the spirit of Greece still breathes and where, two years earlier, I had come to worship some god I no longer knew.

What do I mean by 'only effort'? How could I be interested in myself other than as a perfectible being? Never had my will felt so excited as when straining towards this unknown perfection which I could figure only vaguely in my mind. I used this will exclusively to strengthen and bronze my body. Near Salerno, leaving the coast, we came to Ravello.

There the keener air, the lure of the rocks with their hidden nooks and crannies, the unexplored depths of the valleys all contributed to my strength and my joy, stimulated my enthusiasm.

Nearer to the sky than it is to the sea, Ravello stands on a steep hill overlooking the flat, distant coast of Paestum. During the Norman occupation it was a fairly important town. Now it is merely a narrow village, and we were, I think, the only outsiders. We stayed in a hotel which had formerly been a church house. Situated at the lip of a rock, its terraces and garden seemed suspended in space. Beyond the vine-covered wall all one could see was the sea; one had to go up to the wall to see the cultivated slopes which, by steps rather than paths, connected Ravello to the shore. The mountains continued above Ravello. Huge olive and carob trees, with cyclamen growing in their shadow; above, woods of chestnut trees, cool air, northern plants; below, lemon trees by the sea. The last are arranged in small terraces because of the slope, like a staircase of gardens, almost all the same, with a narrow path running through the middle from end to end. One enters them silently, like a thief. There one can dream, in the green shadows. The foliage is dense and heavy, no direct light can penetrate. The fragrant lemons hang like thick drops of wax; in the shade they look greenish-white; they are within reach, and taste sweet, sharp, refreshing.

The shadows beneath the trees were so dense I dared not stop there while still perspiring from my walk. Yet the steps no longer wore me out. I practised climbing them with my mouth closed. I took less and less frequent rests. I would say to myself, 'I'll get as far as there without giving in.' Then, once I had achieved my goal, I would feel a glow of pride. I would breathe long and deep, which seemed to force the air into my lungs more efficiently. Once again, I was dedicating myself to the care of my body. I was making progress.

I was sometimes surprised at how quickly I was getting better. I began to think that I must have exaggerated the seriousness of my condition, to doubt that I had been very ill, to laugh about the blood-spitting, to regret that my recovery had not been harder.

At first, unaware of the needs of my body, I had not taken good care of myself. I now made a patient study of these needs and became so

ingenious in the exercise of my care that I began to treat it as a game.
What I still suffered from most was my delicate sensitivity to the smallest
change of temperature. Now that my lungs were better, I attributed
this hyperaesthesia to the nervous disorder left over as an after-effect
of my illness. I resolved to conquer this. Seeing the peasants working
in the fields, their beautiful, bronzed, sun-ripened skin showing through
their open jackets, inspired me to get a tan like theirs. One morning,
I undressed and looked at myself. The sight of my pitifully thin arms,
my shoulders slumped forward despite all my efforts and especially the
whiteness, or rather the colourlessness, of my skin, filled me with tears
of shame. I got dressed quickly and, instead of going down to Amalfi,
as I usually did, I headed for some mossy, grass-covered rocks far off
the beaten track, where I knew I wouldn't be seen. When I got there,
I undressed slowly. The air was almost crisp, but the sun was hot. I
exposed my whole body to its rays. I sat up, lay flat, turned over. I
could feel the hard ground beneath me; I was brushed by the waving
grass. Although I was sheltered from the wind, every gust gave me a
quiver of excitement. Soon I felt an exquisite burning all over; my
whole being surged up into my skin.

We stayed at Ravello for a fortnight. I went to the rocks every
morning to continue my cure. Soon the excess layers of clothing I was
still wearing began to feel cumbersome and superfluous. My toned skin
no longer sweated all the time and was able to protect itself with its
own heat.

One morning towards the end of our stay (this was now the middle
of April), I was even more daring. In a gulley in the rocks I have been
telling you about there flowed a clear mountain stream. In fact it formed
a waterfall there – not a very big one, I admit, but it had hollowed out
a pool at its base which was filled with deep, clear water. I had been
there three times and lain flat on the bank, looking into it thirstily,
longingly. I had gazed at its bed of polished rock, where there was not
a mark or a weed to be seen, only the glimmers of dappled sunlight.
By the fourth day I had made my mind up. I went down to the water,
which was clearer than ever before, and without a moment's thought
dived straight in. I soon felt cold, so I climbed out and lay down on
the grass in the sun. There was some wild mint growing there. I picked

some, crushed the sweet-smelling leaves between my fingers and rubbed them over my damp but burning body. I gazed at myself, no longer with shame, but with joy. I felt, if not exactly strong, then at least potentially so, harmonious, sensuous, almost beautiful.

VII

So, in place of all other activity or work, I was content to undertake physical exercise. Clearly this was a change of tack for me, but I really only regarded it as a form of training, a means to an end, rather than something satisfying in itself.

I did something else, which you might find ridiculous, but which I'll tell you about anyway, as it illustrates, in its childish way, my need to find an outer expression for the changes to my inner self: at Amalfi I had a shave.

Until then I had sported a full beard, but had my hair closely cropped. It had never occurred to me that I could change my hairstyle. Then all of a sudden, the first day I went to sunbathe on the rocks, I found my beard irritating. It was like a final piece of clothing I couldn't remove. It felt like a false appendage. It was neatly trimmed – not in a point, but square – and it suddenly struck me as both ugly and ridiculous. Back at the hotel, I looked at myself in the mirror and didn't like what I saw. I looked like what I used to be: a dusty old scholar. Straight after lunch I went down to Amalfi, my mind made up. It is only a small town, I had to make do with a little booth in the square. It was market day, the shop was full, I had to wait for ages. But nothing – the dubious razors, the discoloured shaving brush, the smell, the barber's remarks – was going to put me off. As the scissors snipped away at my beard it was like having a mask removed. However, when I saw myself afterwards, the feeling that filled me, and which I did my best to suppress, was not joy, but fear. I'm not criticizing the way I felt, I merely state it. I thought I looked handsome enough . . . no, my fear came from my feeling that my thoughts were exposed for all to see, and they suddenly seemed quite formidable to me.

My hair, on the other hand, I allowed to grow.

So that is all that my new self found to do in its idle leisure. I thought I would be surprising myself with the enormity of my own actions. But I told myself that would come later, when my new self was more fully formed. Compelled to live a life of waiting, I adopted, like Descartes, a provisional mode of behaviour. This way Marceline would not necessarily notice anything. No doubt the new look in my eye and the change in my expression, especially the day I turned up without my beard, might have worried her somewhat, but by now she loved me too much to see me in my true light. Besides, I did my best to reassure her. It was important that she didn't interfere with my new self-awareness. To shield it from her view, I had to dissimulate.

For the person she loved, the person she had married, was not my 'new self'. I reminded myself of that as a spur to keep it hidden. Thus I offered only an image of myself, which, as time went on, became more and more false.

So for now my relationship with Marceline remained the same – though our love deepened as time went on. My very dissimulation (if that is the right word to describe my need to shield my thoughts from her judgement), my dissimulation helped it to grow. I mean that this game required me to be constantly aware of Marceline. At first, perhaps this necessity to lie required a certain effort, but I soon came to realize that the things which are supposed to be the worst (like lying, to name but that) aren't really difficult at all, except when one has never done them before; in no time at all they become easy, enjoyable; one can do them again without compunction, and very soon they become second nature. Thus, as with anything where one has to overcome an initial revulsion, I began actually to enjoy this dissimulation. I would prolong it, as if to give my new, unknown faculties a chance to play. And I moved forward each day towards a richer, fuller life and a more delicious happiness.

VIII

The road from Ravello to Sorrento is so magnificent that that morning I did not care to see anything more beautiful on earth. The roughness of the sun-warmed rocks, the rich, limpid air, the smells made me feel so alive; so satisfying was it that my only feeling was one of light happiness. Memories and regrets, hopes and desires, past and future all fell silent. Life was nothing other than what came and went with each passing moment. 'O joy of the body!' I exclaimed to myself. 'The steady rhythm of my muscles! Good health!'

I had set off early in the morning, ahead of Marceline, for her overly peaceful happiness would have attenuated my joy, just as her slower pace would have held me back. She would come on by coach to Positano, where we would meet for lunch.

I was nearly at Positano when the sound of carriage wheels, clattering like the bass rhythm of some strange song, made me turn round sharply. At first I couldn't see anything, because of a bend in the road where it swept around the side of a cliff. Then suddenly a coach came into view, travelling at a crazy speed – it was Marceline's. The coachman was singing at the top of his voice, waving his arms about, standing up from his seat and whipping his frightened horse with all his might. The brute! I only just managed to get out of the way as he hurtled past. He didn't stop when I called out . . . I ran after him, but the coach was going too fast. I was terrified that Marceline might jump out of the coach, and equally terrified that she might not. If the horse stumbled she could be thrown into the sea . . . Suddenly the horse fell to the ground. Marceline jumped down and tried to run off, but I caught up with her. When the coachman saw me he unleashed a stream of abuse. I was livid with this man. When he started to insult me I threw myself at him and hauled him down from his seat. We rolled over together on the ground, but I kept the upper hand. He seemed stunned by his fall, and that wasn't helped by the punch in the face I gave him when he tried to bite me. I didn't let go of him, however – I pinned him down by placing my knee on his chest as I attempted to pinion his arms. I looked at his hideous face which my punch had rendered even more ugly. He was spitting, drooling, bleeding, swearing. Oh, what a foul creature! Really! He deserved to have his neck wrung – perhaps I should have done it . . . I certainly felt capable of doing it. I do believe only the thought of the police prevented me.

I finally managed, not without difficulty, to tie the raving lunatic up. I threw him into the coach like a sack.

Ah, what tender looks, what kisses we exchanged after that. I hadn't been in any great danger, but I had had to show my strength, and do so in order to protect her. I felt that I could have given my life for her – and given it gladly . . . The horse had got to its feet. Leaving the back of the carriage to the drunk, we climbed on to the box together and drove the best we could to Positano, then on to Sorrento.

That night, for the first time, I possessed Marceline.

You understand, don't you, or do I need to say it again, that I was a novice in matters of love? Perhaps it was the novelty that gave our wedding night such grace . . . For, in my memory, it is as if that first night were the only one, so much does the expectation and the surprise of love add to the delicious pleasure of the experience – great love needs only a single night to express itself, and my memory insists on recalling that one night alone. It was a single moment which entwined both our souls in its laughter . . . But I believe that love reaches a certain pitch once and once only, which the soul ever after seeks in vain to surpass; that in striving to resurrect that happiness, it actually wears it out; that nothing is more fatal to happiness than the memory of happiness. Alas, I remember that night . . .

Our hotel was outside the town and surrounded by gardens and orchards. Our room opened out on to a very wide balcony, brushed by the branches of the trees. The dawn flooded in through our wide-open casement window. I sat up carefully and tenderly leaned across to Marceline. She was asleep; she seemed to be smiling in her sleep. In contrast to my greater strength she looked so delicate, her grace seemed to be a form of fragility. My head span with a tumult of thoughts. I thought she really meant it when she said I was everything to her. I thought, 'What do I do to make her happy? I abandon her almost all day, every day. She expects everything from me, and I neglect her! . . . Oh, poor, poor Marceline! . . .' My eyes filled with tears. In vain I looked for excuses in my former illness: did I need such constant care now? Was such selfishness appropriate? Wasn't I the stronger of us two now? . . .

The smile had left her lips. The dawn light, which turned everything golden, made her look sad and pale. Perhaps the approach of morning triggered my anxiety. 'Will I have to take care of you one day, Marceline, worry about you?' a voice inside me cried out. I shivered, and gripped by love, pity and tenderness I gently planted between her closed eyes the most tender, loving and pious of kisses.

IX

The few days we spent at Sorrento were peaceful and full of joy. Had I ever known such rest, such happiness? Would I ever again? . . . I was constantly by Marceline's side. I paid less attention to myself and more to her and found as much enjoyment in talking to her as I had previously in keeping to myself.

I was perhaps surprised when I realized that she regarded our nomadic existence as nothing more than a temporary state of affairs. I had declared myself fully content with it. But at the same time I recognized that it was an idle way of life. I accepted that it had run its course and for the first time I felt a desire to work re-emerging from the very inactivity that had enabled me to re-establish my health. I began to talk seriously about going home. From Marceline's look of joy I realized she had been thinking about it for a long time.

However, as I began to consider possible historical projects I realized that they no longer held much attraction for me. As I have already said: since my illness, an abstract, neutral cognizance of the past had struck me as futile. Whereas before I could research philology – for example, attempting to define the Gothic influence in the corruption of Latin – and simply leave aside or overlook the admirable passions of Theodoric, Cassiodorus and Amalasontha in order to concentrate on mere signs, the residue of their lives, now these same signs, indeed philology as a whole, were nothing more than a means of penetrating more deeply into those elements of savage grandeur and nobility that I was beginning to discover. I resolved to delve further into this era; I would limit myself for now to the last years of the Gothic empire, and put to good use our forthcoming visit to Ravenna, the site of its death throes.

But I admit that the figure of the young king Athalaric was the one that attracted me the most. I pictured this boy of fifteen, secretly inspired by the Goths, rebelling against his mother Amalasontha, kicking against his Latin education, rejecting his culture like a horse shaking off a troublesome harness and choosing the society of the uncivilized Goths over that of the old and wise Cassiodorus; for a few years, with a band of rough fellows of his own age, he led a life of violence and unbridled pleasure, only to die at the age of eighteen, burned out by debauchery. In his tragic impulse towards a more savage and unsullied state I found elements of what Marceline would call with a smile 'my crisis'. I thought it was justifiable to take a cerebral approach to the subject, as there was no physical involvement. And I did my best to persuade myself that there was a lesson to be learned in the terrible death of Athalaric.

Before going to Ravenna, where we would stay for a fortnight, we would do a quick tour of Rome and Florence. Then, by missing out Venice and Verona, we would curtail the end of our journey and not stop until we reached Paris. Discussing the future with Marceline gave me a new sort of pleasure. We were still undecided about what we were going to do in the summer. We were both tired of travelling and I needed total peace and quiet for my studies. We thought about a family estate lying between Lisieux and Pont-L'Évêque, in the green Normandy countryside. It had belonged to my mother, and I had spent a few childhood summers there, but had not returned since her death. My father had entrusted the upkeep of the place to a manager, now getting on in years, who collected the rents and sent them on to us on a regular basis. I had delightful memories of a large, pleasant house standing in a garden crossed by streams. The place was called La Morinière. I thought it would be a good idea to stay there.

I talked of going back to Rome the following winter – not as a tourist this time, but to work . . . But this plan was quickly changed: there was a backlog of important mail waiting for us at Naples which included a letter informing me in so many words that my name had been mentioned several times in connection with a chair that had recently fallen vacant at the Collège de France. It was only an acting professorship, but it would leave me free for other things in the future. The friend who had sent me the news pointed out a few steps I might take if I was interested in the post – he was very keen that I should accept it. I hesitated at first, seeing it as a form of bondage, but then began to think that it might be interesting to set out my research on Cassiodorus in a course of lectures . . . The pleasure this would give Marceline is what decided me in the end, and once I had made my mind up, I could see nothing but the advantages.

My father had various contacts in the academic communities of Rome and Florence, with whom I myself had exchanged correspondence. They gave me everything I needed to undertake my research, in Ravenna and elsewhere. I was no longer thinking of anything but work. Marceline quietly encouraged me with her constant kindness and attention.

Our happiness during the final part of our journey was so equable, so peaceful, that there is nothing I can say about it. The finest works of mankind are universally concerned with suffering. How would one tell a story about happiness? One can only tell of the origins of happiness and its destruction. So far, I have told you of the origins.

SECOND PART

I

We arrived at La Morinière at the beginning of July, having stayed in Paris only long enough to do some shopping and to visit one or two people.

As I have said, La Morinière lies between Lisieux and Pont L'Évêque, in the shadiest, wettest countryside I know. Swathes of rolling hills and narrow valleys sweep down to the vast plain of the Vallée d'Auge, which stretches away to the sea. There is no horizon – copses, filled with mystery, a few fields, but largely meadows, gently sloping pastures where the lush grass is cut twice a year, where the ubiquitous apple trees fuse into a single mass of shadow when the sun goes down and where herds of cattle are left to graze at their leisure. Every hollow is filled with water – ponds, pools, streams: the sound of running water is everywhere.

Ah, how familiar the house looked! Its blue roofs, its walls of brick and stone, its moat, the reflections on the still water . . . It was an old house, big enough to sleep twelve. Marceline and three servants, with a little help from me, had their work cut out to make it shipshape. Our old manager, whose name was Bocage, had already prepared a few rooms as well as he could. The old furniture emerged from its sleep of twenty years. Everything was the same as I remembered it; the wainscoting wasn't in too bad a state, the rooms were comfortable enough to live in. To make us feel more welcome, Bocage had filled every vase he could find with flowers. He had had the main courtyard and the park paths nearest the house weeded and raked. When we arrived, the sun was just setting over the house and a mist had gathered in the valley in front of it, alternately masking and unveiling the stream. Just before we reached the house, I suddenly recognized the smell of the grass; and when, once again, I heard the piercing cries of the swallows swooping around the house, the whole of my past, as if it had been lying in wait, rose up to envelop me as I approached.

After a few days the house was in a more or less comfortable state. I could have got on with my work, but I put it off: I was still listening to the myriad small reminders of my past. Then I had a new emotion to deal with: a week after our arrival, Marceline announced that she was pregnant.

I realized that from now on I would have to give her even more care and attention, that she would require more affection than ever. In the period following her announcement, at least, I spent almost every moment of the day by her side. We would go and sit by the wood, on a bench where I used to sit with my mother. There, each moment felt especially delicious, the day went by imperceptibly. If I can't single out any distinct memories of that time, it is not because it was any less vivid, but rather because everything melded together into a uniform sense of well-being: morning flowed into evening, days flowed by without interruption.

I gradually got back to work, my mind calm, alert, sure of its strength, looking to the future with confidence, free of fever, as if my will had been mollified, as if I were heeding the counsel of this temperate land.

I felt sure that this land, where everything was coming to fruition, ready for harvest, was bound to exert a very good influence on me. I looked forward to the tranquil future promised by these sturdy bulls and plump cows in their opulent meadows. The apple trees planted in rows along the favourable slopes of the hills looked set to yield a bumper crop this year; I dreamed of their branches bowing down with their rich burden of fruit. From this ordered abundance, this joyful labour, this happy cultivation a harmony emerged, not by chance but by design, a rhythm, a beauty that was both human and natural, where the bursting fecundity of nature and the skilful regulation of man were so bound together, so in tune with one another, that one no longer knew which one found the most admirable. What would this human effort be, I thought, without the power of the wildness it sought to tame? What would the force and vigour of this wild profusion be without the intelligent effort which channels it and so joyfully extracts such wealth from it? And I imagined a land where all forces would be so regulated, all expenditure so rewarded, all exchanges so strict that the smallest waste would be noticeable. Then, applying my dream to reality, I formed an ethical system which became a science of the perfect utilization of one's self by a controlled intelligence.

So where was my former turbulence? Where had I hidden it? I felt so calm that it was as if it had never existed. The tide of my love had submerged it . . .

Meanwhile, old Bocage bustled around us, offering directions, supervising, giving advice. His need to appear indispensable was becoming very trying. To keep him happy, I had to examine his accounts and listen to his interminable, long-winded reports. Even that wasn't enough: I had to accompany him on his tours of inspection round the estate. His pomposity, his constant prattle, his obvious self-satisfaction, his ostentatious displays of honesty soon drove me to distraction. He became more and more demanding, and I would have given anything to have my peace back. Then an unexpected event transformed the nature of our relationship: one evening, Bocage announced that he was expecting his son Charles to arrive the next day.

I said 'Oh!', rather indifferently, since it hadn't really crossed my mind that Bocage had any children. Then, noticing that he was disappointed by my response, that he was expecting some show of interest or surprise, I added, 'Where is he at present?'

'On a model farm near Alençon,' Bocage replied.

'Let's see, he must be about . . .' I pretended I was working out the age of this son who I didn't even know existed until a moment before, talking slowly enough to give him the chance to dive in . . .

'Just turned seventeen,' said Bocage. 'He was barely four when my lady, your dear mother, died. Oh, he's a big, strapping lad now. He'll soon know more than his father . . .' Once he got started, there was no stopping him, no matter how obvious I made my boredom.

I had forgotten all about it the next day when Charles, newly arrived, came to pay his respects to Marceline and me. He was a handsome fellow, so blooming with health, so lissom and well-made, that even the dreadful city clothes he was wearing in our honour didn't make him look too ridiculous. If anything, his bashfulness merely added to his fine, rosy complexion. He looked about fifteen, with his bright, child-like eyes. He was articulate, devoid of false modesty, and, unlike his father, did not speak when he had nothing to say. I can't remember what we said that first evening; I was too busy looking at him to say much, and left it to Marceline to do the talking. But the following day, for the first time, I went to the farm, where I knew some repair work had just begun, without waiting for Bocage to come and fetch me.

The repairs were being done to a large pond – almost a lake – which was leaking. The leak had been located and now needed to be plugged with cement. Before that could happen, the pond had to be drained, something that hadn't been done for fifteen years. It was full of carp and tench, some of them quite large, which lived at the bottom of the pond. I wanted to stock the moat with some of them, and give the workers some of the rest. So the day's work was to be something of a fishing party, hence the unusual air of excitement around the farm. A few children had come from the surrounding area to join the workers. Marceline was due to come a little later.

Much of the water had been drained before I arrived. Occasionally, a large ripple played across the surface and the brown backs of the disturbed fish came into view. Children paddled in the puddles left at the sides catching small fry, which they threw into buckets containing fresh water. The muddy water in the pond, stirred up by the thrashing of the fish, became more and more of a soup. The number of fish exceeded our expectations. Four farm labourers, plunging their hands in at random, hauled them out. I was sorry that Marceline hadn't come and I was about to run and fetch her when the workers started shouting that they had found eels. No one could catch them, they slipped through their fingers. Charles, who, until that point, had been standing on the bank next to his father, couldn't resist any longer. He quickly pulled off his shoes and socks, threw his jacket and waistcoat to the ground, rolled up his sleeves and his trouser legs and waded purposefully into the ooze. I immediately followed suit.

'Well, Charles,' I called out, 'you must be pleased you came home yesterday.'

He didn't reply, but merely smiled at me; he was already absorbed in his fishing. I called him over a short while later to help me trap a large eel; we joined hands to capture it . . . After that one, we went for another one. Our faces were splashed with mud. In places the water was deeper and we sank in up to our thighs; soon we were wet through. During all this excitement we scarcely exchanged more than a few words and shouts. But at the end of the day, I was aware I was addressing Charles in the familiar form, though I couldn't remember when I had started. We had learned more about each other through our active day together than we would have done through hours of conversation. Marceline hadn't turned up, and never did, but I was no longer regretting her absence. I think she would have taken the edge off our enjoyment.

The very next day, I went to find Charles at the farm. We headed off together towards the woods.

I didn't know my land very well, something which didn't much bother me, but I was astonished to see how familiar Charles was with the estate and the apportionment of the tenancies. He told me I had six tenant farmers, a fact of which I was barely aware, which meant I ought to be earning sixteen to eighteen thousand francs in rent; the fact that I made barely half of that was because of outgoings in sundry maintenance costs and payments to agents. The odd way he smiled as he inspected the crop fields suggested to me my lands were not being exploited to their full potential as I had initially thought, and as Bocage had made out. I pressed Charles on this point and I found his practical way of looking at things, which so exasperated me in his father, entertaining in one so young. We walked together day after day. The estate was huge, and once we had explored every corner, we started again more systematically. Charles barely disguised his annoyance when he saw badly cultivated fields, patches of land overgrown with broom, thistles and weeds. He imparted to me his dislike for fields left fallow and inspired me to think about a better regulated system of farming.

At first I said to him, 'But who loses out from this mismanagement? The farmer alone, surely? However much his income varies, my rent stays the same.'

And Charles got a little annoyed. 'You don't know anything,' he said boldly – which made me smile. 'You're thinking only of your revenue and you fail to notice that your capital assets are deteriorating. If your lands are not farmed well, they gradually lose their value.'

63

'If they could bring in more by being better cultivated, I'm sure the farmers would have done something about it. They wouldn't miss a chance to get as a big a harvest as they can.'

He continued, 'You're not taking into account the extra labour costs. These fields are often a long way from the farms. Cultivating them wouldn't bring in any more, at least not much. But at least they wouldn't go to pot . . .'

And so the conversation went on. Sometimes we would go over the same thing for an hour at a time as we wandered through the fields. But I listened and, little by little, I learned.

'After all, this is your father's responsibility,' I said to him one day, impatiently. Charles blushed a little.

'My father is old,' he said. 'He has enough to do with overseeing the upkeep of the buildings and collecting the rent. It is not his job to make reforms.'

'What reforms would you yourself suggest?' I continued. But then he became evasive and feigned ignorance. I had to twist his arm to get him to be more forthcoming.

'If the farmers leave any land uncultivated, take it away from them,' he finally advised. 'If the farmers leave part of their fields to lie fallow, it proves that they have more than they need to pay you. If they claim they need it all, raise their rents.' And he added, 'They are all lazy around here.'

Of the six farms I owned, the one I liked to visit the most was situated on a hill overlooking La Morinière. It was called La Valterie. The farmer who ran the place was quite pleasant and I enjoyed talking to him. Nearer to La Morinière was a farm known as the 'home farm', which was half-sublet according to a system that left Bocage, in lieu of the absent landlord, in possession of a part of the herd. Now that I had my doubts, I began to suspect honest Bocage himself, if not of cheating me, then of allowing others to take advantage of me. It is true that one stable and one cow-shed were reserved for me, but it occurred to me that they were only there to allow the farmer to feed his horses and cattle on my oats and hay. So far, I had listened indulgently to the implausible reports Bocage gave me from time to time concerning deaths, deformities and diseases, and taken them at face value. I didn't realize that one of the farmer's cows only had to fall ill for it to become my cow, that one of my cows only had to be doing well for it to become one of his. However, after a few careless remarks by Charles and a few observations of my own, the scales began to fall from my eyes. Once I had been alerted, I was not slow to work things out.

At my suggestion, Marceline pored over the accounts, but did not uncover any anomalies. Bocage's honesty was writ large for all to see. What could I do? Let him carry on, but at least now, swallowing my annoyance, I would keep an eye on the livestock, without making it too obvious what I was doing.

I had four horses and six cows – more than enough to cause no end of problems. One of my four horses was still known as 'the colt', even though it was three years old. It was now being broken in. I began to take an interest when, one fine day, I was informed that it was totally unmanageable – there was nothing to be done about this and the best thing would be to get rid of it. In case I should be in any doubt, they made it break the front of a cart and cut its hocks in the process.

On that occasion I found it very difficult not to lose my temper – the only thing that stopped me was Bocage's embarrassment. After all, he is weak rather than wilful, I thought. It's the men's fault – but they don't have any leadership.

I went out into the yard to see the colt. I found a man beating it, but he began to stroke it instead when he heard me coming. I didn't know much about horses, but this seemed like a fine colt to me. It was a very slender half-breed bay with bright eyes; its mane was nearly blond, as was its tail. I made sure it hadn't been injured, asked for its cuts to be dressed and left without another word.

When I saw Charles that evening I tried to find out what he thought of the colt.

'I think he is quite gentle-natured,' he said, 'but they don't know how to look after him. They will turn him into a wild thing.'

'How would you handle him?'

'Would Monsieur give him to me for a week? I'll answer for him.'

'What will you do with him?'

'You'll see . . .'

The next day, Charles took the colt down to a corner of the meadow next to a stream, which was shaded by a superb walnut tree. I went down there, accompanied by Marceline. It is one of my most vivid memories. Charles had driven a stake into the ground and tied the colt to it with a rope several metres long. The colt had been very nervous and had apparently struggled for quite some time. After it had worn itself out it calmed down and was now trotting round in a circle. It had an amazing elasticity in its movements, like a dancer. It was a joy to watch. Charles stood at the centre of the circle, leaping over the rope as it passed, speaking to the colt, either to encourage it or calm it down. He had a large whip in his hand, but I never saw him use it. And all of Charles's movements, imbued with his youth and enthusiasm, imparted a fervent air of enjoyment to the proceedings. Suddenly, I don't know how, he mounted the horse. It had slowed down then stopped, he had stroked it a little, then suddenly there he was sitting confidently on its back, holding on lightly to its mane, laughing and bending forward to carry on stroking it. The colt had bucked only slightly; now it was trotting round again, so beautiful, so supple that I felt envious of Charles and told him so.

'A few more days of breaking-in and the saddle won't tickle him any more. Within two weeks he will be tame enough for Madame to ride. He will be as gentle as a lamb.'

He was right. A few days later, the horse allowed itself to be stroked, harnessed and led without any fuss. And Marceline would have ridden it herself if her condition had allowed it.

'You should try it yourself, Monsieur,' Charles said.

I would never have done it on my own, but Charles offered to saddle up another horse from the farm and the pleasure of his company was enough to persuade me.

How grateful I was to my mother for having taken me to riding-school when I was younger! The distant memory of those early lessons stood me in good stead. I didn't feel too out of place in the saddle; after a few moments I overcame my trepidation and felt quite at ease. The horse Charles was riding was sturdier; it wasn't a thoroughbred, but it wasn't too bad-looking. Charles rode it well. We got into the habit of going for a ride every day. We preferred to set off early in the morning, when the grass was still glistening with dew. We rode to the edge of the woods. As we brushed past the dripping hazel trees we drenched ourselves in the showers of water. Suddenly the horizon opened up – it was the vast Vallée d'Auge, a whiff of sea air from afar. We paused for a while without dismounting. The rising sun coloured the mist then began to disperse it. Then we set off at a canter. We stopped at the farm; the working day was just starting and we felt full of ourselves at being up before the workers, to be there looking down on them from on high. Then we quickly took our leave. I got back to La Morinière just as Marceline was rising.

I would come home drunk on fresh air, giddy with the speed of the gallop, my limbs somewhat stiff with a delicious tiredness, my soul full of health, appetite and freshness. Marceline approved and encouraged me in my fantasy. When I returned, still in my gaiters, I would bring the smell of wet leaves to the bed where she lay waiting for me; she told me that she loved this. She listened to me as I told her about our ride, the awakening of the fields, the start of the day's work . . . It was as if she derived as much pleasure from feeling the life in me as from living herself. Soon I was encroaching on this happiness too: we went for longer rides and I never got back before midday.

However, I earmarked, as much as possible, the late afternoons and evenings for the preparation of my course. This was coming along well, and I was thinking it might be worth publishing later on in book form. My life had fallen into an ordered and regular pattern, and I was happy to keep things that way. As if to compensate for this I became increasingly attracted to the primitive culture of the Goths. With a temerity for which I was later to be roundly criticized, my lectures expounded an apology for and affirmation of their uncivilized ways; yet I worked assiduously to control or even suppress any evidence of such in my own life. Just how well-behaved could I be, how foolish?

Two of my tenants came to see me to renew their leases, which were due to expire at Christmas. Custom dictated that I sign a document known as a 'promissory notice of lease'. Bolstered by Charles's advice and encouraged by our daily conversations, I was in a determined mood as I awaited their arrival. They in turn, firm in their belief that good farmers are hard to find, began by demanding a drop in their rent. So they were all the more astonished when I read out the 'promissory notices' I had drawn up myself, in which I not only refused to lower the rent but also repossessed certain plots of land which I had established they were making no use of. They didn't take me seriously at first: I must be joking. What did I want with this land? It wasn't worth anything – if they did nothing with it, it was because the land was unworkable . . . Then, when they saw I meant what I said, they dug their heels in. I too refused to budge. They tried to scare me by threatening to leave. That was just what I had been waiting for. 'Well, go if you want!' I said to them. 'I'm not stopping you.' And I took the documents and ripped them up in front of them.

So I ended up with over a hundred hectares on my hands. For some time I had been planning to put Bocage in overall charge of this land, thinking that, indirectly, it was Charles I was entrusting it to. I was also intending to get involved myself; however, I gave the matter very little thought – in truth, it was the risk of the undertaking that attracted me. The tenants would not be leaving until Christmas – that left us plenty of time to think things through. I told Charles. His delight displeased me, he couldn't disguise it – it made me even more aware of how very young he was. Time was already short – we were at that part of the year when the fields are ready to be ploughed after the first harvests. By a long-established convention, the work of the outgoing tenant overlaps with that of the incoming tenant, the former surrendering his land field by field as he gathers in his crops. I was afraid that the two farmers I had let go might adopt a hostile attitude by way of revenge. As it happened, they acted in a perfectly co-operative manner (only later did I realize how much that worked to their advantage). I made the most of this and, every morning and evening, walked around the land that was soon to come my way. It was the start of autumn and more men had to be taken on to help out with the ploughing and seeding. We had bought harrows, rollers, ploughs. I rode around on my horse, supervising and directing the workers, taking pleasure in ordering everyone about.

Meanwhile, in the neighbouring meadows, the farmers were gathering apples. The fruit fell from the trees and rolled off into the thick grass – there had never been such an abundant crop. There weren't enough pickers, they had to be brought in from nearby villages, hired by the week. Charles and I sometimes amused ourselves by helping out. Some of the pickers hit the branches with sticks to knock the remaining fruit off. We collected the fruit that had fallen of its own accord to one side; it was over-ripe, often bruised or crushed in the long grass -- you couldn't walk through there without trampling it underfoot. A sickly sweet scent rose from the meadow and mingled with the smell of the ploughed earth.

Autumn was advancing. The mornings of the last fine days are the freshest and clearest of all. Sometimes the moisture in the atmosphere turned everything in the distance blue, making it look even further away; every walk seemed like a journey, the landscape had been expanded. Sometimes, however, the unusual clearness of the air brought the horizon closer, made it seem just a wingbeat away. I don't know which induced the greatest languor. My work was more or less completed, or so I told myself in order to justify seeking out distractions. The time I used to spend at the farm I devoted to Marceline. We went out in the garden together. We sauntered slowly, she hanging languidly on my arm. We walked to a bench overlooking the valley, which caught the sun in the afternoon. She had a sweet way of leaning on my shoulder and we sat there until evening, without moving or speaking, feeling the day melt away within us . . . How our love had already learned to wrap itself in silence! Marceline's love was deeper than words could say; sometimes this love was almost painful to me. Like the surface of a calm pond rippled by the wind, her face would show the slightest emotion. She could hear the stirrings of a new, mysterious life within her, and I gazed into her as into a deep, clear pool where there was nothing but love as far as the eye could see. Oh, if this was happiness, I know I wanted to hold on to it, as one tries to hold water as it slips through the fingers, but I could already feel something else alongside this happiness, something which coloured my love, but coloured it with the hues of autumn.

Autumn was advancing. Every morning the grass was wetter, and never dried out completely inside the edge of the wood; at the first hint of dawn, it was white. The ducks in the moat flapped their wings in an agitated manner; sometimes they took off and flew around La Morinière, making lots of noise. One morning they weren't there,

Bocage had locked them up. Charles told me that they did this every autumn around migration time. And a couple of days later, the weather turned: suddenly one evening there was a stormy blast, a great breath of wind from the sea bringing cold and rain from the north and whisking away the birds of passage. The state of Marceline's health, the need to set up a new apartment and the demands of my course would have soon called us back to town anyway; the early onset of winter hastened our departure.

I would have to come back on farm business in November. I was very annoyed to learn of Bocage's arrangements for the winter. He told me he wanted to send Charles back to the model farm, where, he claimed, he still had a lot to learn. I talked to him long and hard about this, put forward all the arguments I could think of, but I couldn't make him change his mind. All he would concede was a small curtailment of Charles's studies to allow him to return a little sooner. Bocage made no bones of the fact that running the two farms would be extremely difficult, but he told me he had two peasants in mind, whom he considered quite trustworthy. They would be partly farmers, partly tenants, partly labourers, an unprecedented arrangement in these parts for which he did not hold out great hopes. But that was what I wanted, he said. This conversation took place towards the end of October. At the beginning of November, we moved to Paris.

II

We took up residence in the rue S——, near Passy. One of Marceline's brothers had found the apartment, and we had been able to view it on our previous visit to Paris. It was much bigger than the one my father left me, and Marceline fretted somewhat, not only about the higher rent, but also about all the other outgoings such a place would entail. In response to her fears I made out that I hated the thought of being rootless. I even convinced myself of this and deliberately exaggerated it. Admittedly the costs of setting up home exceeded our income for that year, but our fortune was looking healthy and would surely grow further. For this I was counting on my lectures, the publication of my book and – foolishly – the new profits from the farm. I therefore spared no expense, thinking that each outlay entailed a further responsibility which would suppress any wanderlust I might feel – or feared I might feel.

At first we went shopping every day, from dawn till dusk, and even though Marceline's brother very kindly offered to help out, Marceline soon began to feel quite worn out. Then, once we had moved in, instead of getting the rest she needed, she had to play host to an endless stream of visitors. Because we had been away up until then, they flocked along in their droves, and Marceline, who was unused to society, didn't know how to get rid of them or how to prevent them from coming in the first place. I would find her in a state of exhaustion when I came home in the evening. Her fatigue didn't worry me – it was only natural – but I did do my best to alleviate it by receiving visitors in her place, which I didn't much enjoy, and paying visits myself, which I hated even more.

I have never been good at small talk. The frivolity of the salon, the

repertee, none of this had much appeal to me. I had frequented such circles in the old days – but that now seemed so long ago! In company I felt dull, gloomy, anti-social, at once embarrassing and embarrassed . . . By a singular misfortune, you, whom I consider to be my only true friends, were away from Paris and not due to return for a long time. Would I have been able to talk to you any more openly? Would you have been able to understand me better than I did myself? But what did I know then of this thing growing inside me, which I am telling you about today? My future seemed sure, and I had never felt so in charge of it.

And even if I had been more perspicacious, what recourse against myself could I have found in Hubert, Didier, Maurice and all the others of whom you hold the same opinion as I? I'm afraid I soon realized how impossible it was that they should understand me. From our earliest exchanges I felt compelled to act out a false part, to be like that person they thought me still to be, so as not to appear to be pretending. To make things easier, I pretended to have the thoughts and tastes they attributed to me. One can't simultaneously be sincere and be seen to be sincere.

I slightly preferred the company of my colleagues – the archaeologists and philologists – but found talking to them scarcely more enjoyable than flicking through a good historical dictionary. I had hopes initially that certain novelists and poets I knew might offer a more direct understanding of life, but if they had this understanding, they didn't show it. I got the impression that they didn't live at all; they were content merely to give the appearance of it; to them life seemed little more than an annoying impediment to their writing. I couldn't blame them for that. I'm not saying the mistake wasn't mine . . . After all, what did I mean by 'living'? That's exactly what I was hoping they could tell me. Everyone was good at talking about day-to-day events, but no one ever looked at what motivated them.

As for the philosophers, who, by definition, should have been in a position to impart some wisdom, I had long ago learned to expect little from that quarter. These mathematicians and neo-Kantians tried to remain as detached as possible from the troubles of real life and had as much interest in it as the algebraist has for the object of his calculations.

When I came home to Marceline, I did nothing to conceal the boredom these visits caused me.

'They are all the same,' I told her, 'like exact copies. When I speak to one I could be speaking to any of them.'

'But my love,' Marceline replied, 'you can't expect them all to be different.'

'The more they are like each other, the less like me they are.' And I went on sadly, 'None of them has been ill. They are alive, they give the appearance of living, yet they don't seem to know they are alive. Come to that, since I've been in their company, I haven't been alive myself. Today, for example, what have I done? I had to leave you at nine o'clock this morning. Before I went I just had time to read a couple of pages. That is the only good thing that has happened all day. I met your brother at the solicitor's and then couldn't get rid of him. He came with me to the upholsterer, made a nuisance of himself at the cabinet-maker's, and I didn't manage to shake him off until we got to Gaston's. I had lunch in that part of town with Philippe, then met Louis in a café. Together we sat through an absurd lecture by Théodore, which I afterwards praised. In order to get out of his invitation for Sunday, I had to accompany him to Arthur's. With Arthur we went to a watercolour exhibition. Then I dropped off some cards at Albertine's and Julie's . . . I come home exhausted and find you are just as tired as I am from seeing Adeline, Marthe, Jeanne, Sophie . . . And now that I look back on my day it all seems so pointless and empty that I wish I could have it back again and relive it and it just makes me want to cry.'

Yet I was incapable of saying what I meant by 'living', or whether the taste I had acquired for a life which was more airy and spacious, less confined and less geared towards the demands of others, might not be the simple reason for my unrest. The real reason seemed to me much more mysterious than that. It was that I had come back from the dead, I thought. I was a stranger among ordinary people like a man who has risen from the grave. At first I felt disturbed and confused. But soon I became aware of a totally new feeling. As I have said, I felt no pride when the work for which I received so much praise was published. Was this pride I was feeling now? Perhaps, but at least there was no

73

hint of vanity mixed in with it. For the first time I was aware of my true worth. The very things that separated me and distinguished me from other people were what mattered; the very things no one else would or could say, these were the things I had to say.

My lectures began shortly after this. I was carried along by my theme, and infused my first lecture with my new passion. Referring to the end of the Latin civilization, I represented artistic culture as a type of secretion welling up within a people, at first indicating a plethora, an abundance of health, but later congealing, solidifying, forming a hard membrane preventing direct contact between spirit and nature, creating an appearance of vitality which disguises the decline of life within, like a casing in which the spirit languishes, wilts and finally dies. Pushing these thoughts to their natural conclusion, I made the assertion that Culture, which is born of life, ends up killing it.

Historians accused me of overgeneralization. Others criticized my methods. And those who complimented me were the ones who had understood me the least.

It was after my lecture that I first bumped into Ménalque. I had never known him well, and shortly before my marriage he had set off on one of his expeditions which would sometimes take him away for more than a year at a time. I had never liked him much before – he seemed rather haughty and showed no interest in knowing me. So I was surprised to see him at my first lecture. The same insolence that had formerly put me off now appealed to me, and the smile he gave me seemed all the more charming, given that he was someone who smiled rarely. He had recently been involved in an absurd, shameful lawsuit, and the newspapers had taken advantage of the scandal to blacken his name; people he had offended with his contemptuous manner took advantage of the situation to exact their revenge. The fact that he seemed little affected by this only served to infuriate them further.

'One has to allow people to be in the right,' he replied to all the insults. 'It's some consolation for the fact that they don't have anything else.'

However, 'decent society' was outraged and so-called 'respectable' people felt impelled to turn their backs on him and pay him back for his contempt in kind. To me this was another point in his favour. Attracted by some secret affinity between us, I went up to him and embraced him warmly in front of everyone.

When they saw who I was talking to, the last of the hangers-on dispersed and I was left alone with Ménalque.

After all the annoying criticisms and inept compliments, his comments on my lectures were reassuring.

'Everything you once held in such high esteem you've thrown on the bonfire,' he said. 'A little late in the day, perhaps, but the flame burns all the more brightly for that. I'm still not sure I understand you; you intrigue me. I'm not one for idle chat, but I wouldn't mind talking with you. Dine with me this evening.'

'My dear Ménalque,' I replied, 'you seem to forget I am married.'

'Oh yes,' he responded, 'so you are. From the warmth of your welcome I might have thought you still single.'

I was worried that I had offended him. I was even more worried that I might have appeared feeble, so I agreed to meet him after dinner.

As he was just passing through Paris, Ménalque was staying in a hotel. For the duration of his stay he had had a number of rooms set up as an apartment. He had his own servants, took his meals apart, lived apart; he had covered the walls and furniture, whose banal ugliness he found offensive, with expensive hangings he had brought back from Nepal. He was wearing them in, he claimed, before giving them to a museum. Such was my haste to see him that he was still eating when I arrived. I apologized for disturbing his meal, but he said, 'I have no intention of letting you disturb my meal, and I trust you will allow me to finish it. If you had come to dinner I should have offered you some Shiraz, the wine that Hafiz sang about, but it's too late now. It must be drunk on an empty stomach. Would you accept a liqueur instead?'

I accepted, thinking that he would join me, but I was surprised when they brought only one glass.

'Excuse me,' he said, 'but I rarely drink.'

'Are you afraid of getting drunk?'

'Oh no,' he replied. 'Quite the opposite. It's just that I find sobriety a more powerful form of intoxication, one where I retain my lucidity.'

'And you offer drinks to others . . .'

He smiled.

'I can't expect others to share my virtues,' he said. 'It's good enough for me if they share my vices . . .'

'You smoke, at least?'

'Not any more. It's an impersonal, negative sort of intoxication which is achieved too easily. I seek to heighten life, not diminish it, through intoxication. Let's change the subject. Do you know where I've just been? Biskra. I knew you had recently been there and I wanted to follow in your footsteps. What was he up to in Biskra, this blinkered scholar, this bookworm? It is my custom to be discreet only when confided in; as for things I find out for myself, I must admit my curiosity knows no bounds. So I rooted around and asked questions wherever I could. My indiscretion has done me a favour, as it has kindled the desire to see you again, for instead of the bookish stick-in-the-mud of old, I now know you to be . . . well, you tell me.'

I felt myself blush.

'What exactly did you find out about me, Ménalque?'

'Do you really want to know? Don't worry! You know your friends and mine well enough to know there is no one I can talk to about you. You saw how well your lecture went down!'

'But,' I said slightly impatiently, 'I have seen nothing yet to prove that I could talk to you any more than I could talk to the others. Tell me, what did you find out about me?'

'First of all, that you had been ill.'

'But what's that got to do . . .'

'Oh, it's actually quite important. Then I was told that you went out on your own, without a book (that's what made me wonder), or, when you weren't alone, that you preferred being with children rather than your wife . . . Don't blush, or I won't tell you the rest.'

'Don't look at me then.'

'One of these children – his name was Moktir, if memory serves me, an uncommonly handsome lad and the finest little crook I have ever come across – seemed to have a lot to say about you. I enticed him, bought his trust – not easy, as you know; I'm sure he was lying even when he said he wasn't lying . . . Tell me whether what he said about you is true.'

Ménalque had stood up and had taken a small box out of a drawer, which he then opened.

'Are these your scissors?' he asked, handing me a mangled, blunt, rusty object, which I nevertheless had no difficulty in recognizing as the little pair of scissors that Moktir had pinched.

'Yes, they are, they belonged to my wife.'

'He claims that he took them from you when you had your back turned, one day when you were alone in the room together. But what is really interesting is that he also claims that, as he was hiding them away inside his *burnous*, he realized you were watching him in the mirror and he caught your eye in the reflection. You had seen him steal the scissors and said nothing! Moktir was most surprised that you kept silent, as, indeed, was I.'

'As am I at what you've just said. You mean he knew that I had spotted him?'

'That's beside the point. You were trying to beat him at his own game – when it comes to cunning, these children will always come out on top. You thought you had him, but in fact he was the one who had you . . . No, that is not the point. Tell me why you didn't say anything.'

'I'd like to know the reason myself.'

Neither of us spoke for a while. Ménalque paced up and down the room, absent-mindedly lit a cigarette, then stubbed it out straight away.

'You don't seem to have a sense,' he continued, 'of what other people would call the "value of things".'

'We're talking about "moral value", I suppose,' I said, forcing myself to smile.

'No, simply the value of possessions.'

'You don't strike me as having much yourself.'

'So little that nothing in this apartment belongs to me – not even, or should I say especially not, the bed I sleep in. I hate resting. Possessions encourage this; when one feels secure one falls asleep. I love life enough to prefer to live it awake. So within all this wealth I preserve a sense of precariousness with which I aggravate, or at least intensify, my life. I can't claim that I love danger, but I do like life to be risky, I like it to make demands on my courage, my happiness, my health at every moment . . .'

'So what are you criticizing me for?' I interrupted.

'Oh, you misunderstand me, my dear Michel. Just as I was being foolish enough to attempt a profession of faith! . . . I care little for the approval or disapproval of others, so I am not likely to sit in judgement myself. These terms are meaningless to me. I have been speaking too much about myself – I was too eager to make myself understood . . . I simply wanted to say that, for someone with no sense of property, you seem to own quite a lot. And that is a serious matter.'

'And what is this vast property I'm supposed to possess?'

'Nothing, if you take it that way . . . Aren't you getting on your high horse a little? Don't you own an estate in Normandy? Haven't you just moved into a rather luxurious apartment in Passy? You're married. Aren't you expecting a child?'

'Well!' I snapped impatiently. 'That merely proves that I have managed to court more "danger" – to use your word – in my life than you have in yours.'

'Quite, "merely",' said Ménalque, ironically. Then he turned round sharply and offered me his hand.

'Well, goodbye. That's enough for this evening – this isn't really getting us anywhere. But I hope to see you soon.'

I didn't see him again for quite a while.

I had other things to keep me busy. An Italian scholar told me about some new documents he had discovered and I had to study them in detail for my course. The poor reception given to my first lecture had spurred me to adopt a different approach and argue my case more powerfully in the ones that followed. This led me to assert in a more dogmatic fashion what I had previously only hazarded as an ingenious hypothesis. How often does the force of one's assertions derive from the fact that one's subtle suggestions fall on stony ground! In my case I can't honestly say what proportion of this understandable need to assert my case was sheer pig-headedness. The new things I had to say seemed all the more pressing, the more trouble I had in saying them and having them understood.

But how pale are mere words compared to actions! Wasn't Ménalque's life, his smallest action, a thousand times more eloquent than
my lectures? Now I understood that the moral lessons of the great
philosophers of Antiquity were given as much by example as by words,
if not more so.

The next time I saw Ménalque, almost three weeks after our first
encounter, was at my house. It was at a rather overcrowded party, and
he made his appearance towards the end. Marceline and I had an 'open
house' every Thursday evening as a way of avoiding having to receive
people the rest of the week. Every Thursday, our self-styled friends
would come over. We had the space to cater for a large crowd, and
the party would go on well into the night. I think they were mainly
drawn by Marceline's exquisite charm and the pleasure of talking among
themselves, for by the second of these soirées I had run out of things
to say, could no longer be bothered to listen and was barely able to
disguise my boredom. I would drift from the smoking-room to the
drawing-room, from the antechamber to the library, occasionally catching something someone said, observing little of what was going on but
looking round in a desultory fashion.

Antoine, Étienne and Godefroy were discussing a recent vote in
Parliament as they sprawled on my wife's delicate armchairs. Hubert
and Louis were carelessly manhandling some etchings from my father's
collection. In the smoking-room Mathias had left his lit cigar on top
of a rosewood table as he listened attentively to Léonard. Someone had
spilt a glass of curaçao on the carpet. Albert had taken the liberty of
putting his feet up on one of the sofas, and was dirtying it with his
muddy shoes. The very air we breathed was full of the dust of all this
wear and tear . . . I had a sudden urge to kick the lot of them out.
Furniture, fabrics, prints lost all value for me once they were stained –
these stains were like the taint of illness, the mark of death. I wished I
could protect everything, keep it under lock and key for myself and
myself alone. I thought how lucky Ménalque was to own nothing. I
end up suffering from my need to preserve everything. But in the end,
what does it really matter? . . .

In a small, dimly lit room to the side, separated by a glass door,

ANDRÉ GIDE

Marceline was talking to a few close friends. She was reclining on some
cushions, and looked so terribly pale and tired that I felt very worried
and decided there and then that this would be the last party we would
give. It was already quite late. I was reaching into my waistcoat pocket
for my watch when I felt Moktir's little scissors.

'So why did he steal them,' I thought, 'only to ruin them straight
away?'

At that moment someone tapped me on the shoulder. I turned round
immediately. It was Ménalque.

He was almost the only person in evening dress. He had only just
arrived. He asked me to introduce him to my wife – I certainly
wouldn't have done so of my own accord. Ménalque was elegant,
almost handsome, with a face like a pirate, divided in two by an
enormous, tumbling moustache, greying at the edges. The cold flame
of his gaze suggested courage and decisiveness rather than goodness.
No sooner had I presented him to Marceline than I realized that she
didn't take to him. I let them exchange a few banal pleasantries, then
took him off to the smoking-room.

I had learned only that morning that the Ministry for the Colonies
was entrusting him with a new mission. A number of newspapers
reviewed his adventurous career to date, conveniently forgetting that
they had been insulting him only very recently, and struggled to find
words fine enough to sing his praises. They vied with each other to
extol the services rendered to the state, to humanity as a whole, by the
strange discoveries he had made on his recent expeditions, as if he had
been driven purely by humanitarian motives. And they lauded his
qualities of self-denial, dedication and boldness, as if such panegyrics
were to be considered rewards in themselves.

I started to congratulate him, but he interrupted me before I could
get the words out.

'Not you too, my dear Michel!' he said. 'At least you didn't insult
me in the first place. Leave all that nonsense to the newspapers. They
seem surprised to discover that someone with a questionable reputation
can also have virtues. I cannot recognize such distinctions and reser-
vations, for I exist as a single whole. My only claim is to be natural; if
something gives me pleasure, I take that as a sign that I should do it.'

'That can have consequences,' I said.

'I certainly hope so,' Ménalque replied. 'If only all these people here could see the sense of that. But most of them believe the only good comes from restraint; their pleasure is counterfeit. People don't want to be like themselves. They all choose a model to imitate, or if they don't choose a model themselves, they accept one ready-made. Yet I believe there are other things to be read in a man. No one dares. No one dares turn the page. The law of imitation – I call it the law of fear. They fear finding themselves alone, so they don't find themselves at all. I detest this moral agoraphobia, it is the worst form of cowardice. He who invents must do so alone. But who here is trying to invent? The things one feels are different about oneself are the things that are rare, that give each person his value – and these are the things they try to repress. They imitate, and they make out they love life!'

I let Ménalque talk. He was saying the very same things I myself had said to Marceline a month before, so I should have agreed with him. So for what reasons of cowardice did I interrupt him and repeat, word for word, what Marceline had said when she interrupted me?

'But my dear Ménalque, you can't expect them all to be different . . .'

Ménalque was silent all of a sudden. He gave me a strange look, then, when Eusèbe came over to say goodbye, unceremoniously turned his back and went off to talk to Hector about nothing in particular.

I realized what I had said was stupid the moment I said it. I especially regretted that I might have given Ménalque to believe that I felt threatened by what he had said. It was late, my guests were leaving. When the drawing-room was almost empty, Ménalque came back to me.

'I can't leave it like this,' he said. 'I must have misunderstood what you said. Allow me at least that hope . . .'

'No,' I replied, 'you didn't misunderstand me . . . but what I said was meaningless. No sooner had I said it than I regretted my stupidity. The worst thing was the feeling that I was aligning myself with the very people you were attacking, whom, I assure you, I loathe as much as you. I hate all people of principle.'

'There is nothing more contemptible,' Ménalque replied, laughing.

'They don't possess an ounce of sincerity, for they only ever do what their principles decree or, failing that, see what they do as wrong. The slightest hint that you might be one of them froze me in mid-sentence. The sadness this caused me revealed to me how strong my affection for you is. I hoped I was mistaken – not in my affection, but in the conclusion I came to.'

'You did indeed jump to the wrong conclusion.'

'Did I, indeed!' he said, grabbing my hand. 'Listen. I will be going away soon, but I would like to see you again. This trip will be longer and more hazardous than the others; I don't know when I will return. I leave in a fortnight. No one else knows that I am leaving so soon, it's a secret I'm sharing with you. I leave at dawn. The night before a journey is always one of terrible anxiety for me. Prove to me that you are not a man of principle: can I count on you to spend this last night with me?'

'But we will see each other before then,' I said, somewhat surprised.

'No. During the next fortnight I will see no one. I won't even be in Paris. Tomorrow I leave for Budapest. Within a week I should be in Rome. There are friends all over to whom I must bid farewell before I leave Europe. One of them is in Madrid . . .'

'Very well, I will spend that night of vigil with you.'

'And we will drink the wine of Shiraz.'

A few days after this party Marceline began to feel less well. I have already told you that she was often tired, but she never complained, and as I attributed this tiredness to her condition, it didn't cause me undue concern and I thought no more about it. A foolish – or rather, ignorant – old doctor had reassured us that there was nothing to worry about. However, Marceline developed further symptoms and became feverish, so I decided to call in Dr Tr—, who was meant to be the top specialist in this field. He was surprised that I hadn't called him sooner and he prescribed a strict diet which Marceline should really have started much earlier. Marceline had recklessly been pushing herself too hard; from now until the birth, which was due at the end of January, she was to put her feet up. I'm sure Marceline was more anxious and poorly than she would care to admit, and she submitted meekly to all the doctor's instructions, however irksome they were. She did, however, show some resistance when Tr— prescribed quinine in doses which she knew could be dangerous to the baby. She refused to take any for three days, but her fever got worse and she had to acquiesce to this too, albeit with a heavy heart, as if she were renouncing all hope for the future. She resigned herself in an almost religious fashion; her will, which had sustained her up until that point, was undermined, so much so that her condition took a significant turn for the worse in the few days that followed.

I looked after her with greater care than ever and reassured her the best I could, reminding her that Tr— had said he didn't think her condition was critical. But the strength of her fears soon alarmed me in turn. Oh, how precariously our happiness still relied on sheer hope and an uncertain future! As someone who was once interested only in the past, I thought, I might have been intoxicated by my first real taste of the present moment; but the future can strip the present of its charm more than the present does to the past. And since that night in Sorrento I had been pinning all my love, my whole life, on the future.

Nevertheless, the evening I had promised to spend with Ménalque came round, and notwithstanding my unwillingness to leave Marceline on her own for a whole winter night, I did my best to make her understand the importance of the occasion and the gravity of my promise. Marceline was feeling a little better that evening, but I was still concerned. I had a nurse sit at her bedside in my place. But no sooner had I left the building than my anxiety grew stronger. I suppressed it, struggled against it, berated myself for not being able to overcome it. I managed to work myself up into a state of high tension, a strange excitement at once very different from and very like the painful anxiety that had produced it, but even closer to happiness. It was late, I was striding out, the snow began to fall more heavily. I felt happy to be breathing at last a sharper air, to be battling against the cold; I felt happy in the wind, the dark, the snow. I savoured my own energy.

Ménalque heard me coming and appeared on the landing to meet me. He seemed impatient. He looked pale and tense. He took my coat and made me take off my wet boots and put on some soft Persian slippers. Some food had been laid out on a pedestal table next to the fire. There were two lamps in the room, but most of the light came from the fire. Ménalque asked after Marceline. I decided to keep it simple and told him she was fine.

'Your baby must be due quite soon?' he went on.

'In a month's time.'

Ménalque leant over towards the fire, as if trying to hide his face. He didn't say anything. He stayed silent for so long I began to feel embarrassed, as I didn't know what to say to him either. I got up and walked away a little, then came back and laid my hand on his shoulder. As if speaking his thoughts aloud, he murmured, 'One has to choose. The main thing is to know what one wants . . .'

'You mean you don't want to go?' I asked, unsure how to read what he had said.

'It seems that way.'

'Won't you change your mind?'

'What would be the point? You can stay, with your wife and child . . . There are thousands of ways of life and each of us can know only one. It's madness to envy other people's happiness. Happiness doesn't come off the peg, it has to be made to measure. I leave tomorrow. I know – I have tried to tailor this happiness to fit me . . . You hang on to the comfortable happiness of home life.'

'I have also tailored my happiness to fit,' I cried out. 'But I have grown, and now my happiness is too tight. Sometimes it almost strangles me . . .'

'Bah, you'll manage!' said Ménalque. Then he planted himself in front of me and looked deep into my eyes. As I couldn't find anything to say, he smiled a little sadly. 'We imagine we possess, but in truth we are possessed. Pour yourself some Shiraz, dear Michel, you won't taste that every day. Try some of these pink sweets which the Persians eat with it. This evening I want to drink with you, forget that I am leaving in the morning and talk as if the night would last for ever . . . Do you know why poetry and especially philosophy are so lifeless these days? It is because they are detached from life. The Greeks created their ideals directly from life. The life of the artist was itself an act of poetic creation, the life of the philosopher an enactment of his philosophy. Both were bound up with life: instead of ignoring each other, philosophy fed poetry and poetry expressed philosophy, with admirably persuasive results. Nowadays beauty no longer appears in action, action no longer aspires to be beautiful, and wisdom exists in a separate sphere.'

'But you live your wisdom,' I said. 'Why don't you write your memoirs? Or simply,' I went on, seeing him smile, 'your recollections of your travels?'

'Because I don't wish to remember,' he replied. 'It would be like forestalling the future and allowing the past to encroach upon me. I create each hour anew only by completely forgetting the past. I am never content simply *to have been* happy. I don't believe in dead things. For me, being no more is the same as never having been.'

His words were beginning to irritate me, they were so far in advance of my own thoughts. I wanted to rein him back, stop him in his tracks, but I couldn't come up with an argument against anything he said. Besides, I was more angry with myself than with Ménalque. So I remained silent as he paced up and down like a caged beast, sometimes stopping to lean over the fire, sometimes saying nothing for ages, then suddenly breaking into speech:

'If only our mediocre brains were able to embalm our memories! But they aren't easy to preserve. The most delicate ones shrivel away, the more voluptuous ones rot. The most delicious ones are the most dangerous in the long run. The things one repents of are the things that were delicious when they happened.'

There was another long silence, then he continued, 'Regrets, remorse, repentance: past joy, seen in retrospect. I don't like to look back, I leave my past behind as a bird leaves its shade when it takes flight. Oh, Michel, joy is out there waiting for us, but it always wants to find the bed empty, to be the one and only; it requires us to come to it free of attachments. Oh, Michel, joy is like manna in the desert, which goes stale after a day. It is like the water from the fountain of Ameles, which, as Plato tells us, no vase can contain . . . Every moment should take away with it everything it brings.'

Ménalque talked for a long time. I can't tell you everything he said, but much of it made a deep impression on me, especially those things I would rather have drawn a veil over – not that he taught me anything I didn't know, but he stripped bare my own thoughts, thoughts I had

ANDRÉ GIDE

buried under layers of disguise, as if trying to smother them. And so
the vigil passed.

The next morning, after I had seen Ménalque off at the station, I
made my lonely way home to Marceline with a feeling of deep sadness
and intense hatred for Ménalque's cynical form of joy. I wanted to
believe it was all a sham, I was desperate to deny it. I was annoyed that
I hadn't said anything in reply. I was annoyed that I had said some
things that might have led him to doubt my happiness, my love. And
I clung tight to this dubious happiness, my 'comfortable happiness', as
Ménalque had put it. I couldn't dispel a feeling of unease, but I convinced
myself that this unease could nourish my love. I concentrated on the
future and could already see the smiling face of my little baby. The
thought helped to stiffen my morale . . . I was positively striding out
now, full of confidence.

Alas, when I got home, I was met by a scene of unprecedented chaos
the moment I stepped through the door. The nurse came out to see
me and, choosing her words carefully, informed me that my wife had
suffered severe anxiety attacks during the night, and had been in some
pain, though she didn't think she was about to go into labour. She had
felt very ill and had sent for the doctor. Though he had arrived in the
middle of the night, he had not yet left his patient's side. The nurse
must have seen me turn pale, for she tried to reassure me, telling me
that she was already showing signs of improvement, that . . . I rushed
into Marceline's room.

The room was dimly lit. At first I could only make out the doctor,
who signalled to me to be quiet, then, in the darkness, a figure I didn't
recognize. Anxiously, without a sound, I approached the bed. Marceline
had her eyes shut. She was so dreadfully pale that at first I thought she
was dead. But, without opening her eyes, she turned her head towards
me. In a dark corner of the room the unknown person was arranging
various objects and putting them away. I saw gleaming instruments,
cotton wool. I saw, I thought I could see, a cloth stained with blood
. . . I felt my legs give way. I almost fell into the doctor's arms – he
held me up. I realized with a sense of dread what had happened.

'The baby?' I asked anxiously.

He shrugged his shoulders sadly. Without knowing what I was doing,

86

I threw myself on the bed, sobbing. How suddenly the future had arrived! The ground gave way beneath my feet, a yawning hole opened in front of me, and I staggered headlong into it.

My memories at this point all fuse into one dark mass. However, at first Marceline seemed to get better quite quickly. It was the New Year holiday, so I was able to be with her almost every hour of the day. As I sat with her, I read or wrote, or else read aloud to her. Whenever I went out I brought her back flowers. I remembered how well she had cared for me when I was ill, and I tended her so lovingly that it sometimes made her smile, as if she were happy. Not a word was said about the tragic accident that had shattered our hopes . . .

Then she had an attack of phlebitis. Then, as that was clearing up, an embolism brought her to the brink of death. It was night-time. I can still see myself now, leaning over her, feeling my own heart stop and start again with hers. How many nights I spent like that, watching over her intently, hoping that the strength of my love would force some of my life into her. I rarely thought of happiness now, my only sad pleasure was seeing Marceline smile occasionally.

My course was about to start again. Where would I find the strength to prepare and give my lectures? . . . I have difficulty remembering this time, I forget how the weeks went by. There is, however, one thing I wish to tell you about.

It was one morning shortly after the embolism. I was sitting with Marceline, who seemed a little better. But she was still under doctor's orders to lie perfectly still – she wasn't even allowed to raise an arm. I was giving her something to drink, and when she had finished and I was still leaning over her, in a voice made even weaker by her emotion, she begged me to open a small box which she indicated to me with her eyes. The box was on the table; I opened it. It was full of ribbons, scraps, small trinkets. What was she after? I carried the box over to the bed and took out its contents one by one. Is this it? Or this? . . . No, keep looking. I could see she was getting a little worried.

'Oh, Marceline, it's this rosary that you want.' She tried to smile. 'Are you afraid I'm not looking after you well enough?'

'Oh, my dear,' she murmured. And I recalled our conversation in

Biskra, and her fearful reproach when she heard me reject what she called 'God's help'.

I continued, somewhat roughly, 'I managed to get better on my own.'

'I prayed for you so much,' she replied, in a voice that was both tender and sad. She had an anxious, imploring look in her eyes . . . I picked up the rosary and slid it into her hand, which lay limply by her side on the covers. She thanked me with a tearful, loving look, to which I felt unable to respond. I hesitated a moment, unsure of what to do, feeling awkward. Finally, I couldn't bear it any longer.

'Goodbye,' I said, and left the room, bristling with hostility, as if I had been banished.

However, the embolism had caused serious complications. The awful clot of blood which the heart had ejected caused congestion in her lungs and impeded her breathing, making it short and laboured. I didn't think I would see her well again. The illness had entered into her and taken up residence; it marked her, stained her. She was damaged beyond repair.

III

It was turning milder. As soon as my course came to an end, I took Marceline to La Morinière. The doctor had advised that she was out of danger and only needed fresh air to help her get better. I was greatly in need of some rest myself. I had been worn out by the long vigils next to her bed, which I had insisted on keeping myself, the prolonged anxiety and especially the sympathetic symptoms I had experienced at the time of her embolism, when the spasmodic beat of her heart was echoed in mine. I felt as if I had been ill myself.

I would rather have taken Marceline to the mountains, but what she really wanted most of all was to go back to Normandy. She claimed that no other climate would suit her better and she reminded me that I had to take a look at the two farms I had so rashly taken under my wing. She argued that, as I had taken on the responsibility, I owed it to myself to ensure that they were a success. No sooner had we arrived than she sent me out to inspect the estate . . . I suspect that behind her gentle insistence was a great deal of self-sacrifice, that she feared that the demands her illness was making on me might be causing me to feel trapped . . . However, Marceline was feeling better; she was getting the colour back in her cheeks, and nothing gave me greater comfort than to see her smile less sadly. I was able to leave her without worrying.

So I went to visit the two farms. It was the start of haymaking. The air was full of pollen, of scents, and it went to my head like strong drink. It was as if I hadn't breathed for a year, or else had been breathing nothing but dust, so smoothly did the honey-sweet air fill my lungs. As if intoxicated, I had sat down on a bank and now had a panoramic view of La Morinière. I could see the blue roofs, the still water of the moat; surrounding it, the newly mown fields, and others still full of grass; further away, the bend of the stream, the woods where I had gone riding with Charles last autumn. I could hear singing, and it was getting closer; it was the haymakers on their way home, their pitchforks and rakes slung over their shoulders. The sight of these workers, most of whom I recognized, gave me an unwelcome reminder that I wasn't here as an enraptured traveller but as their master. I went over, gave them a smile, talked to them, inquired after each of them at length. Bocage had already given me a report on the state of the crops that morning; indeed, he had been sending regular letters keeping me up to date with every little thing that had been happening on the farms. Things were going quite well, much better than Bocage had initially led me to expect. However, they were waiting for me to make one or two crucial decisions, and for a few days I tried to take charge of things as best I could, albeit without any great relish, seeking some solace in this semblance of work for the failures of my life.

When Marceline was well enough to receive visitors, we had a few friends to stay. Their gentle, quiet company was just what Marceline needed, but their presence made me all the more ready to go out. I preferred the company of the farm workers; I felt I had more to learn from them – not that I was quizzing them all the time – and I can't really express the joy that their company gave me. It was as if I could feel things through them – whereas I knew what our friends were going to say even before they opened their mouths, the mere sight of these poor people constantly filled me with wonder.

Though at first they responded to my questions with the condescension I strove to avoid in my own manner when I talked to them, they soon learned to put up with me. I had more and more contact with them. Not content with following them in their work, I wanted to see them at play. I wasn't too interested in hearing their obtuse opinions, but I joined in their meals, listened to their jokes, fondly observed their pleasures. By some sympathetic process similar to the one that caused my heart to stutter alongside that of Marceline, I felt an instantaneous echo of every strange sensation – not a vague one, but precise, sharp. I could feel the mower's stiffness in my arms, I felt tired with his tiredness; the cider he drank quenched my thirst, I felt it slide down his throat. One day, one of them cut his thumb while sharpening his scythe; I felt the pain jab me to the bone.

It was as if I learned about this land not only with my eyes, but also *felt* it in some tactile way which this strange sympathetic sense rendered more acute.

Bocage's presence bothered me. When he was about I was forced to play the master, which I didn't like at all. I still gave orders – I had to – and directed the workers in my own fashion, but I no longer rode around on my horse, for fear of lording it over them. Though I took pains to ensure that they wouldn't feel inhibited by my presence, I still felt a wicked curiosity about them. The existence of every single one of them was a mystery to me. It seemed there was always some part of their lives which remained hidden. What did they do when I wasn't there? I couldn't quite believe that they didn't have better ways of amusing themselves. I fancied they all had some secret, which I was determined to uncover. I hung around, followed them, spied on them. The more uncultured they were the better – I peered into their darkness as if expecting some ray of illumination to emerge.

I was drawn to one of them in particular. He was tall and quite handsome, not unintelligent, but guided entirely by his instincts. Everything he did was on the spur of the moment – he only ever acted on impulse. He wasn't a local, he was simply here because he happened to have been hired for work. He would work diligently for two days, then drink himself half to death on the third. One night I sneaked up on him in the barn; he lay sprawling in the hay in a drunken stupor. I stayed there for a long time, looking at him . . . One fine day he left just as he had arrived. I wished I knew which route he had taken . . . That evening I learned that Bocage had sacked him.

I was furious with Bocage. I summoned him.

'It appears that you have sacked Pierre,' I said. 'Can you tell me why?' He was somewhat taken aback by my anger, though I had done my best to attenuate it.

'I didn't think Monsieur would want to retain a filthy drunk like him. He was a bad influence on the other men . . .'

'I think I am best placed to judge whom I wish to retain or not.'

'A wastrel, sir. We don't even know where he came from. That sort of thing doesn't go down well in the country . . . Perhaps it would have made Monsieur happy if he had burned the barn down one night.'

'Well, that's my business. I seem to recall that this is my farm, and I intend to run it as I please. In future, if you wish to fire someone, I want to hear your reasons first.'

As I have said, Bocage has known me since I was a child. However hurtful my tone, he was too fond of me to take any real offence. In fact, he didn't take me seriously enough. The Norman peasant is unwilling to believe anything if he can't see the reason behind it – in other words, if it is not in his interest. As far as Bocage was concerned, I was just in one of my moods.

Nevertheless, I didn't want to end our conversation on this note. I felt I had been too sharp with him, and wondered what I could say to patch things up. After a moment or two's silence, I hit upon:

'Will your son Charles be coming back soon?'

'I thought Monsieur had forgotten all about him, since he has hardly asked after him at all,' said Bocage, still rather hurt.

'Me, forget all about him? How could I, Bocage, after all we did together last year? I have him very much in mind for the farms, as it happens . . .'

'Monsieur is too kind. Charles is coming home in a week's time.'

'Good, I'm glad, Bocage.' And I dismissed him.

Bocage wasn't too wide of the mark: I certainly hadn't forgotten Charles, but I barely thought about him. How was it that, after such an exciting friendship, I could now scarcely summon up any interest in him at all? The fact was that my tastes and interests had changed since last year. I had to admit that my two farms were of less interest to me than the people in my employ. If I was to go on frequenting them, Charles's presence was going to be an impediment. He was far too sensible and respectable. So, despite the quiver of excitement his memory evoked in me, I was dreading his imminent return.

He arrived. Oh, my fear that Ménalque was right to repudiate all memory was not misplaced! In place of Charles there entered an absurdly pompous figure in a bowler hat. My God, how he had changed! Despite my embarrassment, I tried to not react too coldly to his evident joy at seeing me again; but even his joy displeased me – it was gauche and came across as insincere. I had received him in the drawing-room, and, as it was late, I couldn't make out his features very well. But when a lamp was brought in, I saw to my disgust that he had let his side-whiskers grow.

We had a thoroughly dreary conversation that evening. Then, as I knew he would always be hanging round the farms, I didn't go down there for a week – instead, I fell back on my studies and the society of my guests. Then, when I started to go out again, I had new matters to occupy me.

The woods were full of woodcutters. The woods were divided into twelve equal sections, and each year timber from one of these plots was sold as firewood – both the twelve years' growth of brushwood and any full-size trees that had stopped growing.

This work took place in winter. The terms of the contract stipulated that the plot had to be cleared before the spring. But such was the negligence of old Heurtevent, the wood merchant in charge of the clearance, that the work would often drag on well into the spring; delicate, fresh shoots would be sprouting among the felled timber, so that when the woodcutters finally cleared the ground, they destroyed many of the new saplings.

This year, Heurtevent's slackness exceeded our worst expectations. In the absence of a higher bid, I had had to let him have the timber at a very low price. With his profit neatly sewn up, he made little effort to dispose of the timber which he had got so cheap. Week after week the work was delayed: first the excuse was the lack of available labour, then it was the bad weather, then a sick horse, cash-flow problems, other jobs . . . heaven knows what else. The result was that by the middle of the summer none of it had been removed.

The previous year, this would have irritated me in the extreme, but this year I remained calm. I wasn't denying that Heurtevent had done me wrong, but I found these ravaged woods quite beautiful. I loved to walk in them, watching the game birds, startling vipers and sometimes sitting for hours on one of the felled trunks, which seemed to be still alive, with green shoots sprouting from its severed end.

Then, around the first week of August, Heurtevent suddenly decided to send some men round. Six of them turned up, claiming they were

93

going to complete the work in ten days. The section of the woods being cleared lay next to La Valterie. To help the work along I allowed the men to be brought their meals from the farm. The man charged with this task was a young rogue by the name of Bute, who had just returned from his military service somewhat the worse for wear – mentally, that is; physically, he was in fine shape. He was the one of my farm hands I most enjoyed talking to. This way I could see him without having to go to the farm. It was just around this time that I started going out again. For several days I was rarely away from the woods; I went back to La Morinière only for my meals, and was often late for them. I pretended that I was supervising the work, but in reality I was interested only in the workers.

Sometimes the six workers were joined by two of Heurtevent's sons. One was twenty, the other fifteen; they were slim, bow-legged, with hard faces. They had a foreign look about them – I found out later that their mother was Spanish. At first I was surprised that someone like her should have ended up here, but it turned out that Heurtevent had been a bit of a wanderer in his youth and had married her in Spain. This was rather frowned upon by the locals. The first time I met the younger son, I seem to recall, it was raining. He was sitting alone on top of a pile of faggots on a high cart. He was reclining among the logs, singing, or rather bawling, a strange song, the like of which I had never heard in these parts. The horses pulling the cart knew the way and didn't need to be driven. I can't tell you the effect this song had on me, for I had heard nothing like it except in Africa . . . The boy was lively, as if drunk. When I went past he didn't even look at me. I learned the next day that he was Heurtevent's son. So I hung around the woods in the hope of seeing him again. The clearance was completed quickly. Heurtevent's sons came only three times. They seemed very aloof and I couldn't get a word out of them.

Bute, on the other hand, loved to tell stories. I soon convinced him that it was safe to tell me anything. From then on he was uninhibited and gave me all the local gossip in intimate detail. I listened eagerly to all his secrets. He surpassed my expectations, yet at the same time left me feeling dissatisfied. Is this what was lurking below the surface? Or was it just another layer of hypocrisy? No matter! I probed Bute as I had the primitive chronicles of the Goths. His stories gave off vapours of the abyss; I inhaled them uneasily, feeling my head spin. It was from him that I learnt that Heurtevent slept with his daughter. I feared that, if I displayed the slightest disapproval, he might clam up. So I smiled, driven by curiosity.

'What about the mother? Hasn't she said anything?'

'The mother! She's been dead for a good twelve years . . . he beat her.'

'How many of them are there?'

'Five children. You've seen the oldest and the youngest sons. There's one who's sixteen – a bit of a weakling, wants to be a priest – and the eldest girl already has two children by the father . . .'

I gradually learned other things about the Heurtevents that made their house sound like a stinking den of depravity. Despite my best efforts, my imagination was drawn to it like a fly to rotting meat. One evening the eldest son tried to rape a servant girl. She put up a struggle, so the father came to his son's aid and held her down with his massive hands. This all took place while the second son was upstairs saying his prayers and the youngest, who was playing near by, looked on. I don't think the rape itself can have been too difficult, for it seemed that the girl acquired a taste for that sort of thing and a short time afterwards tried to seduce the young priest.

'Did she succeed?' I asked.

'He's still holding out, but his resistance is weakening,' Bute replied.

'Didn't you mention another daughter?'

'She's anybody's – and for free. If she's really keen, she wouldn't mind paying for it herself. But don't do it at her father's house, you'll get a good hiding. He says you can do what you like in your own home, that's nobody else's business. Pierre, the farm hand you sent away, got a crack on the head there one night, though he's kept his mouth shut about it. Since then she's been doing it in the woods.'

I gave him an encouraging look, and asked, 'Have you done it?'

He lowered his eyes for the sake of modesty and chuckled.

'Sometimes,' he said. Then, raising his eyes quickly, he added, 'And so has Bocage's young one.'

'Which young one?'

'Alcide, the one who sleeps at the farm. Doesn't Monsieur know him?'

I was astonished to hear that Bocage had another son.

'I suppose he was still living with his uncle last year,' Bute continued. 'But I'm surprised you've never come across him in the woods, Monsieur. He's out there poaching almost every night.'

He said this last bit in a whisper. He was looking at me intently, and I realized I needed to smile. This satisfied Bute, and he went on.

'Ah, Monsieur knows there are poachers in these woods. They're big enough – it can't do any harm.'

I gave no sign of displeasure, so Bute grew bolder. Looking back, I don't think he was too displeased to be doing Bocage a disservice. He showed me where Alcide had set his traps, then he told me about a place in the boundary hedge where I was virtually certain of catching him red-handed. It was a narrow opening where the hedge ran along the top of a slope; Alcide usually came through there around six o'clock. Bute and I had fine sport: we stretched a copper wire across the opening, which we neatly concealed. Bute made me swear that I wouldn't name him and then went away to avoid being compromised. I lay down on the other side of the slope and waited.

I kept watch there for three nights in a row. I was beginning to think that Bute had played a trick on me when, finally, on the fourth evening, I heard a light step approaching. My heart was pounding, and I suddenly got a taste of the delicious fear a poacher must feel. The trap was so well set that Alcide walked straight into it. I saw him tumble over as his ankle got caught in the wire. He tried to free himself, fell over again and began to struggle like a trapped animal. But by now I had a hold of him. He was a wicked-looking young urchin with green eyes, stringy hair and a sly expression on his face. He kicked out. When I managed to pin him down, he tried to bite me, and when that didn't succeed, he let out the most extraordinary stream of abuse I have ever heard. I couldn't resist any longer – I burst out laughing. This brought him to an abrupt halt. He looked at me, and continued, in a lower voice:

'You've crippled me, you brute.'

'Show me.'

He slid his stocking down over his boot and showed me his ankle, where there was a very faint pink mark.

'It's nothing.'

He gave a little smile, then went on slyly, 'I'll tell my father you've been setting traps.'

'But it's one of yours!'

'Course it is. You didn't set that.'

'Why do you say that?'

'You wouldn't know how. Show me how you did it.'

'You teach me . . .'

That evening I got home late for dinner. No one knew where I had been and Marceline was worried. I didn't tell her how I had laid six traps and, instead of scolding Alcide, had given him six sous.

The next day, when I went with him to check the traps, I found to my amusement that we had caught two rabbits. Naturally, I let him keep them. As the hunting season had not yet opened, I wondered what they did with the game, given that it couldn't be disposed of legally. Alcide wouldn't tell me. In the end I found out, again from Bute, that Heurtevent was a major receiver, and that his youngest son acted as a go-between between him and Alcide. Was this going to allow me greater access to the enclosed world of this mysterious family? I went about my poaching with great zeal!

I met up with Alcide every evening. We caught large numbers of rabbits, and even on one occasion a roe deer. It was still showing faint signs of life when we found it. I still shudder when I think about how much Alcide enjoyed killing it. We placed the dead deer in a safe place where Heurtevent's son would find it in the night.

I was no longer so keen on going out during the day, when the bare woods held less to entice me. I even turned to my work – a sad, pointless exercise, as I had resigned from my post at the end of my course. It was thankless labour, from which I was easily distracted by the sound of someone singing or the slightest noise from the outside world; every voice I heard seemed to be calling me. How often would I drop my book and dash to the window, only to find nothing there! How often would I rush out of the house . . . The only way I could pay attention to anything was through my five senses.

97

But when night fell – and at this time of year night came quickly – our hour had come. I had never known until then how beautiful it was. I slunk out like a thief, I had the eyes of an owl. The grass seemed taller, more alive in the wind, the trees more dense. Everything was exaggerated by the dark: the ground appeared more distant, every surface appeared to have depth. The most even of paths seemed dangerous. All around one could sense the creatures of the night stirring.

'Where does your father think you are right now?'

'Looking after the animals, in the stable.'

I knew Alcide slept there, next to the pigeons and the hens. As he was locked in every night, he got out through a hole in the roof. His clothes still bore the warm smell of poultry . . .

Then once we had gathered in our catch, he would disappear into the night as if through a trapdoor, without waving goodbye, without even saying 'See you tomorrow'. I knew that, before going back to the farm, where the dogs would not bark at his approach, he met up with young Heurtevent and handed over his bounty. But where? I couldn't get it out of him – threats, tricks, none of them worked. I couldn't get near the Heurtevents. I find it hard to say which was the grander folly: chasing some banal mystery that constantly evaded my grasp? Or perhaps inventing this mystery out of sheer curiosity? But what did Alcide do when he left me? Did he really sleep at the farm? Or did he only make the farmer believe that he did? Oh, I had compromised myself in vain. I only succeeded in losing his respect without gaining his trust. It both infuriated me and depressed me at the same time . . .

Once he had left I would suddenly feel terribly alone. I would walk home across the fields, through the dew-sodden grass, drunk on the night, the wildness, the anarchy, soaked through, muddy, covered with leaves. Like a welcoming, distant beacon the light from the lamp in Marceline's room guided me back to the sleeping La Morinière. I had convinced Marceline that I couldn't get to sleep if I didn't make these night-time excursions. It was true: I had grown to hate my bed; I would rather have slept in the barn.

Game was plentiful this year. Rabbits, hares, pheasants in quick succession. On the third evening, when he saw that everything had turned out all right, Bute decided to tag along with us.

On our sixth outing we could find only two of our twelve traps – someone had done a raid during the daytime. Bute asked me for a hundred sous to buy some more copper wire – normal wire was no good.

The next day I had the singular pleasure of seeing my ten traps at Bocage's house. I was compelled to congratulate him on his zealous work. What was really galling was that, the previous year, I myself had offered ten sous for every trap that was found. So I had to give Bocage a hundred. However, Bute bought some more wire with his hundred. But four days later the same thing happened – ten more traps were seized. That meant another hundred for Bute, and another hundred for Bocage.

When I congratulated Bocage, he said, 'It's not me you have to thank, it's Alcide.'

'Really?' I tried to contain my astonishment – I didn't want to give us away.

'Yes,' Bocage continued. 'What can I say, Monsieur? I'm too old for that sort of thing. I'm needed at the farm. The boy scours the woods for me. He knows them so well. He's very sharp. He knows where to find the traps better than I do.'

'I bet he does.'

'So, Monsieur, from the ten sous you give me, I give him five for every trap.'

'I'm sure he deserves it. My word, twenty traps in five days. He has been working hard. The poachers had better beware. I wager they'll be keeping their heads down for a while.'

'Oh, Monsieur, the more we remove, the more we find. Game is fetching a good price this year, so for the sake of a few sous . . .'

I had been so well and truly taken for a ride that I was almost inclined to believe Bocage was in on it. What I found particularly vexing was not Alcide's triple-dealing but the fact that he had deceived me. And what did he and Bute do with the money? I don't know, I will never know anything about these people. They will always lie, they will always cheat me just for the pleasure of it. That evening I didn't give

Bute a hundred sous, I gave him ten francs. I told him that was all he would get, so if more traps were seized, then too bad.

The next day I saw Bocage approach with a worried expression on his face. That made me feel even more worried. What had happened? Bocage told me that Bute had only got back to the farm at dawn. He was as drunk as a lord. When Bocage had tried to say something he had called him some terrible names, then leaped on him and started to punch him . . .

'So I have come to request, Monsieur,' Bocage said, 'that you *authorize* (he stressed the word) me to dismiss him.'

'I'll think about it, Bocage. I am very sorry that he treated you with such disrespect. I'll see . . . Give me a couple of hours to think about it, then come back and see me.'

Bocage left.

If I kept Bute, it would be a slap in the face for Bocage. But if I dismissed Bute, it might incite him to get his own back. Too bad. I would have to cross that bridge when I came to it. I only had myself to blame . . .

When Bocage returned, I said, 'You can tell Bute not to show his face round here again.'

Then I waited. What would Bocage do? What would Bute say? It was not until the evening that I caught the first ripples of scandal. Bute had talked. I surmised this when I heard yells coming from Bocage's house. It was young Alcide receiving a beating. I knew Bocage would come to see me. He did. I heard his doddery old steps approach, and my heart beat faster than it did when I was out poaching. It was unbearable! I would have to listen to a lot of righteous sentiments, I would have to take him seriously. What explanation could I come up with? I was sure I couldn't carry it off. If only I didn't have to play the part . . . Bocage came in. I didn't take in a single word he said. It was absurd – I had to get him to repeat everything. Eventually, I gathered that he believed that Bute alone was guilty. The unbelievable truth passed him by completely – that I had given Bute ten francs. Why? His Norman brain couldn't admit the possibility. Bute must have stolen the ten francs. By claiming that I gave them to him he was compounding his theft with a lie. It was a story he had made up to conceal his crime.

He couldn't pull the wool over Bocage's eyes . . . No mention of poaching. The reason that Bocage had been beating Alcide was simply that he had stayed out all night.

I was off the hook! At least as far as Bocage was concerned, everything was all right. What an idiot Bute was! I certainly had no desire to go out poaching that night.

I thought it was all over and done with. But an hour later Charles turned up. He didn't look as if he was paying a friendly visit. Even from a distance he looked more boring than his father. To think that a year ago . . .

'Hello, Charles, I haven't seen you for a long time.'

'If you are so keen to see me, Monsieur, you only have to come down to the farm. You're not likely to bump into me in the woods at night.'

'Ah, your father told you . . .'

'My father told me nothing, because he knows nothing. Why should he have to know, at his age, that his master is making a fool of him?'

'That's enough, Charles, you're going too far . . .'

'Fine, you're the master! You can do whatever you like.'

'Charles, you know perfectly well that I've made a fool of no one, and if I do what I like, it does no harm to anyone but myself.'

He gave a slight shrug of the shoulders.

'How can we defend your interests if you attack them yourself? You can't protect both the gamekeeper and the poacher at the same time.'

'Why not?'

'Because . . . Oh, all right, you're too smart for me, Monsieur. I just don't like it when my master teams up with the very people we're trying to stop and undoes all the good work we have done for him.'

Charles grew in confidence as he spoke. He almost acquired a certain nobility. I noticed that he had had his whiskers cut. And besides, what he was saying was quite fair. When I didn't reply (what could I say?), he went on:

'Ownership entails certain obligations – you yourself taught me that last year, but you seem to have forgotten it. You must take these obligations seriously and not treat them as a game, otherwise you don't deserve to be a proprietor.'

Silence.

'Is that all you have to say?'

'For now, yes, Monsieur. But in future, if you force my hand, I may well have to inform you that my father and I will be leaving La Morinière.'

He went out, bowing very low. I had no time to think.

'Charles!' He was right, by God . . . But if that was what ownership entailed . . . 'Charles!' I ran after him, caught up with him outside in the dark and told him quickly, as if to seal my peremptory decision, 'You can tell your father that I am putting La Morinière up for sale.'

Charles bowed gravely and left without a word.

The whole thing was totally absurd.

Marceline didn't come down for dinner that evening, but sent word that she felt unwell. Anxiously I ran upstairs to her room. She quickly set my mind at rest. 'It's just a cold,' she said. She thought she had merely caught a chill.

'Couldn't you have wrapped up warm?'

'When I first started shivering, I put on my shawl.'

'You should have put it on before you started shivering, not after.'

She looked at me and attempted to smile. Perhaps it was because the day had got off to such a bad start that I felt so prone to anxiety. She couldn't have made it any clearer if she had come out and said, 'Do you really care so much whether I live or not?' Everything was unravelling around me. Everything was slipping out of my grasp . . . I threw myself at Marceline and covered her pale forehead with kisses. At that she broke down and started sobbing on my shoulder.

'Oh, Marceline, Marceline, let us leave here! We can go somewhere else and I can love you as I loved you in Sorrento. You think I've changed, don't you? But if we go somewhere else, you will see that nothing has altered our love.'

I could not cure her sadness, but how readily she clutched at that straw of hope!

It was not too late in the year, but it was cold and damp and the last of the rosebuds were already wilting before they had opened. Our guests had long since gone. Marceline wasn't so ill that she couldn't organize the shutting-up of the house, and five days later, we left.

THIRD PART

And so I tried, once again, to take a firm hold of my love. But did I really need this peaceful happiness? The love that Marceline gave me, the love that she symbolized for me, was like rest for a man who isn't tired. But as I sensed how exhausted she was, and how much she needed my love, I lavished it on her, pretending that it sprang from my own need. I couldn't bear to see her suffering; I loved her in order to cure her.

Oh, such passionate, tender care! As others breathe life into their faith by exaggerated observance of its practices, so I worked on my love. And Marceline quickly rediscovered her hope: she was still so young, and I promised so much. We fled from Paris as if on a second honeymoon. But on the very first day of the journey, she started to feel ill. By the time we reached Neuchâtel, we had to stop.

I loved this lake, with its blue-green shores, its marshy waters seeping through the rushes and mingling with the land; it was so un-Alpine. I found Marceline a room in a comfortable hotel with a view of the lake. I never left her side all day.

She was so unwell that I called a doctor from Lausanne the following morning. Rather pointlessly, he was keen to ascertain whether I knew of any incidences of tuberculosis in my wife's family. I said I did, even though I knew of none, for I didn't want to tell him that I myself had nearly died of it and that, before she nursed me, Marceline had never been ill. I blamed it all on the embolism, though the doctor insisted that this was just a contributory factor, and the root of the problem lay further back. He heartily recommended the climate of the high Alps, which he assured me would bring her back to health. This fitted with my own intention to spend the whole winter in Engadine, so as soon as Marceline was fit enough to travel, we set off.

I remember all the sensations of that journey as if they were singular events. The air was limpid and cold. We had brought our warmest furs . . . At Coire, we could hardly sleep a wink because of the incessant din in the hotel. I could have put up with a sleepless night and not felt tired, but Marceline . . . it wasn't the noise itself that bothered me so much as the fact that it stopped her getting any sleep. She needed it so much! The next day, we set off before dawn. We had reserved seats in the Coire mailcoach. Thanks to some good connections, it was possible to get to St Moritz in a day.

Tiefenkasten, the Julier, Samaden . . . I remember everything, hour by hour: how the air felt different, colder; the sound of the horses' bells; my hunger; our midday halt at the inn; the raw egg I broke into my soup; the brown bread and the cold, bitter wine. This basic fare wasn't to Marceline's taste – she couldn't eat anything but a few dry biscuits which I had had the foresight to bring with me. I can recall the sunset, the shadows racing up the forested hillsides; then another stop. The air is becoming keener, rawer. When the coach stops, we plunge into the depths of the darkness and a silence that is limpid – that's the only word for it. And against this strangely transparent silence the slightest sound acquires perfect plenitude and resonance. We set off again into the darkness. Marceline coughs . . . Oh, will she ever stop coughing? My mind goes back to the Sousse coach. I'm sure I coughed better than that – she's putting too much into it . . . She seems so weak, so different. In the shadow I hardly recognize her. How drawn her face looks! Were those two black holes of her nostrils always so prominent? Oh, she has an awful cough. It is the most obvious consequence of her care for me. I hate sympathy – behind it lurks infection. One should only sympathize with the strong. Oh, she really is on her last legs! Please let us arrive soon . . . Now what is she doing? . . . She has taken out her handkerchief, she is raising it to her lips, turning her head away . . . The horror! Is she also going to spit blood? I snatch the handkerchief roughly from her hands. I examine it in the half-light of the lantern . . . Nothing. But I have displayed too much anxiety. Marceline forces a sad smile and murmurs:

'No, not yet.'

Finally, we arrived – not before time, for she could barely stay on her feet. The rooms prepared for us were far from satisfactory. We slept there that night, and changed rooms the following day. Nothing seemed nice enough, nothing too expensive. As the winter season had not yet begun, the hotel was almost empty. We were spoiled for choice. I picked two light, spacious, simply furnished rooms with an adjoining sitting-room fronted by a bow window which looked out over the ugly blue lake and a stark mountain whose sides were either too wooded or too bare. We decided to take our meals in this room. The apartment was an exorbitant price, but no matter. I no longer had my teaching post, but I was going to sell La Morinière. Then we would see . . . Besides, what did I need of money? What need did I have of all that? I was strong now . . . I believed a complete change of fortune was as formative as a complete change of health . . . Marceline needed some luxury. She was weak . . . Oh, for her I would spend and spend until . . . And I grew to hate this luxury and yet enjoy it at the same time. I bathed my sensuality in it, then wished that sensuality could be footloose and free.

However, Marceline was getting better. My constant care was proving effective. As she was having trouble eating, I ordered dainty gourmet dishes to whet her appetite. We drank the best wines. I had so much enjoyment experimenting with these exotic wines that I convinced myself that she had developed a real taste for them. We tried sharp Rhineland wines, syrupy-thick Tokays which filled me with their heady goodness. I recall a strange Barba-grisca: I had only one bottle left, so was unable to verify whether its preposterous taste was typical.

Every day we went out for carriage rides. When the snow came, we went out in a sledge, wrapped up to the neck in furs. My face would be glowing red by the time we got back; I would be ravenous and ready for bed. Nevertheless, I hadn't totally abandoned my work, and every day I would set aside at least an hour to meditate on the things I felt I had to say. History didn't come into it any more. For some time now historical research had been of no other interest to me than as a means of psychological inquiry. I have said how I had discovered a new passion for the past when I thought I saw unsettling similarities to the present. I had had the temerity to believe that I could interrogate the dead to make them give up some secret about life . . . Now young

Athalaric himself could have risen from the dead and spoken to me, I was no longer listening. How could Antiquity provide an answer to my new question: what is man still capable of? That was what I needed to know. Is what man has said to date all he is capable of saying? Was there anything about himself he might have missed? Has he nothing left to do other than repeat himself? . . . Every day the feeling grew in me that there were untapped riches to be found hidden under the suffocating layers of culture, decency and morality.

It seemed to me that I had been born to make new sorts of discoveries. I grew strangely excited by my investigation into the darkness, knowing that it entailed a repudiation of all culture, decency and morality.

I began to appreciate other people only when they displayed their wild side; I hated it when they suppressed this out of some sense of restraint. I more or less regarded honesty as a matter of restriction, convention or fear. I would have loved to cherish it as something rare and difficult, but our manners had turned it into something banal, a form of contract. In Switzerland it is a means of making everything comfortable. I realized it was what Marceline needed, but I still didn't conceal the new course my thoughts were taking. Even back in Neuchâtel, when she was full of admiration for the honesty of these people, saying how it seemed to permeate every face, the stones themselves, I retorted:

'My own is more than enough for me. I detest these honest folk. I may have nothing to fear from them, but I have nothing to learn from them either. And they have nothing to say . . . Oh, these honest Swiss. Where do their good manners get them? . . . They have no crime, no history, no literature, no art . . . They are like a sturdy rosebush without thorns or flowers.'

I already knew before coming here that this honest country would bore me. But two months on, this boredom had boiled up into a kind of rage, and I could think of little else but getting away.

It was now mid-January. Marceline was feeling better, much better. The constant light fever that had been sapping her strength had gone away, some colour had returned to her cheeks, she enjoyed walking again, though only a little at a time, and she wasn't permanently tired as she had been before. I didn't have much difficulty in persuading her that she had derived as much benefit as she was going to from the bracing mountain air and that the best thing for her now was to head down to Italy, where the gentle springtime mildness would complete her cure. I didn't have that much difficulty in persuading myself either, so fed up was I of these mountain climes.

Now that the hateful past is sweeping back through my idle present with renewed force, these are the memories that stick in my mind above all others: rapid sleigh-rides, sprays of snow, the joy of the biting cold air, keen appetite; stumbling along in the fog, the distorted voices, objects suddenly looming out of the mist; reading, cosy and warm, in the sitting-room, the view of the landscape out of the window, the icy landscape; the unbearable wait for snow; blotting out the outside world, sinking sensually into one's thoughts . . . Oh, to go skating with her again, just the two of us, on that pure little lost lake in among the larches. Then to come home with her in the evening . . .

The journey down into Italy was as dizzying as a fall. The weather was fine. As we came down into the warmer, denser air, the rigid regularity of the larches and pines of the mountains gave way to a richer, softer, more naturally graceful vegetation. It was like exchanging abstraction for life, and even though it was still winter, I thought I could smell scents everywhere. For too long we had had nothing to enjoy but shadows. I was intoxicated by my privation, drunk on my thirst as others are drunk on wine. I had shown an admirable thriftiness; now, on the threshold of this land of tolerance and promise, all my appetites were bursting into life. I was swamped by a huge reserve of love. Sometimes it surged from the depths of my flesh to my head, filling my mind with dissolute thoughts.

The illusion of spring did not last. The sharp drop in altitude deceived me at first, but once we had left the sheltered shores of the lakes, Bellagiò and Como, where we had stayed for a few days, we ran into wet, wintry weather once again. We had been able to tolerate the crisp, dry cold of the mountains quite well, but down here the damp, heavy air began to take its toll. Marceline's cough returned. We headed further south to escape the cold. From Milan we went to Florence, then to Rome, then to Naples, which in the winter rain is by far the most depressing place I have ever been to. I felt oppressed by some indefinable

ennui. We returned to Rome, hoping to find, if not warmth, then a
modicum of comfort. We rented an apartment on the Monte Pincio
– it was too big for us, but excellently situated. We had had enough of
hotels by the time we reached Florence, and had taken a three-month
lease on a superb villa on the Viale dei Colli. Anyone else would have
been happy to stay there for ever . . . we stayed less than three weeks.
However, wherever we stopped, I took pains to arrange things as if we
were never going to leave. I was driven by some irresistible demon . . .
on top of this, we never had less than eight trunks with us when we
travelled. One of them was full of books, and I never opened it once
during the whole journey.

I didn't consult Marceline on our finances, and I didn't allow her to
try to curb our expenses. I knew that they were excessive, and that we
couldn't go on in this way. I no longer counted on seeing any money
from La Morinière – the income from the estate had dried up and
Bocage had been in touch to say he couldn't find a buyer. But when
I thought about the future, the result was that I spent even more. What
would I need with all this money, I thought, once I was on my own?
. . . And I watched, full of fear and expectation, as Marceline's fragile
life ebbed away even more quickly than my fortune.

Although she relied on me to take care of everything, these sudden
changes of scene tired her out. But what tired her out even more – I
can admit it now – was her alarm at what was going on in my head.

'I understand your doctrine,' she said to me one day, 'for that is what
it has become – a doctrine. And no doubt it is a very fine one.' Then
she added sadly, lowering her voice, 'But it leaves out the weak.'

'That's how it should be,' I replied immediately, in spite of myself,
and I could feel this delicate creature recoil and shudder at the harshness
of my words . . . Perhaps you are thinking that I didn't love Marceline.
I swear to you that I loved her passionately. She had never been so
beautiful – not to my eyes. The illness had made her features more
refined, more other-worldly somehow. I now rarely left her side, I
gave her my constant attention, watched over her day and night. She
slept very lightly, but I trained myself to sleep more lightly still. I
watched her as she went to sleep, and I was the first to wake up. On
the occasions when I left her for an hour to go for a walk in the country

or the town, some kind of lover's anxiety, some fear that she might be languishing without me, always hastened me back to her side. Sometimes I summoned up my will and rebelled against this constriction: I said to myself, 'Aren't you worth more than this, you man of straw?' And I made myself stay out longer. But then I would come home with an armful of flowers, whether early garden blooms or greenhouse flowers ... As I say, I cherished her dearly. But how can I put this ... my veneration of her grew in inverse proportion to my self-respect. And who can say how many passions and conflicting thoughts can coexist within a man?

The bad weather had long since ended, the season was well advanced and suddenly the almond trees were in bloom. It was the first of March. In the morning I went down to the Piazza di Spagna. The peasants had stripped the trees of their white branches and the flower-sellers' baskets were full of almond blossom. I was so enchanted I bought a whole bundle. Three men helped me to carry this mass of spring back home. The branches got snagged in the doorways, showering the carpet with petals. I filled all the vases and put them all round the apartment. While Marceline was out, I turned the drawing-room white. I was already anticipating her joyful reaction ... I heard her coming. She came through the door ... then staggered back and burst into tears.

'What's wrong, my poor Marceline?'

I rushed to her side, covered her mouth with tender kisses.

'The smell of these flowers is making me feel sick,' she said, by way of explanation for her tears ...

There was a faint, very faint, discreet smell of honey ... Without a word, I gathered up all these delicate, innocent branches, broke them up, took them out and threw them away, my head pounding with sheer exasperation – oh, if this slight taste of spring was too much for her! ...

I often think about this tearful episode and I now believe that she already sensed that she didn't have long left and that she was crying tears of regret for other springs. I also believe that there are strong joys for the strong and weak joys for the weak, and that the joys of the strong would be damaging to the weak. The merest drop of pleasure was enough to make her drunk. The slightest increase in intensity would have been too much for her. What she called pleasure I called rest, and I didn't want to rest, I was unable to rest.

Four days later, we set off again for Sorrento. I was disappointed that it wasn't warmer there. The whole place seemed to be shivering. The wind never stopped blowing and it made Marceline feel very tired. We had planned to go back to the hotel where we had stayed on our last visit. We booked the same room . . . But we were astonished to find the place so devoid of charm – under the grey sky, the delightful garden where we had walked as lovers looked dull and ordinary.

We resolved to sail to Palermo, where we had been told the climate was good. We went back to Naples, where we were to embark, and stayed there for a few days. But at least in Naples I no longer felt bored. Naples is a lively town and it had no connections with the past.

I spent nearly every moment of the day with Marceline. She was tired in the evenings and went to bed early. I would watch over her as she fell asleep, and sometimes got into bed myself, but as soon as the regularity of her breathing told me she had gone to sleep, I would get up without a sound, get dressed in the dark and slip out of the house like a thief.

When I got out of the house I felt like dancing for joy. What was I going to do? I didn't know. The sky, which had been overcast all day, was now free of clouds, and the almost full moon shone brightly. I wandered aimlessly, feeling no desire, no constraint. I looked at everything with a fresh eye; I heard every sound with a more attentive ear; I breathed in the dampness of the night; I touched things with my hand; I went prowling.

On our last night in Naples my vagrant spree lasted until dawn. When I got home, I found Marceline in tears. She told me she had felt afraid when she had woken up in the night and realized I wasn't there. I calmed her down, explained my absence as convincingly as I could and promised not to leave her again. But on our very first night in Palermo I couldn't resist the temptation to go out . . . The first orange blossoms were just appearing; the slightest breath of wind carried their scent . . .

We stayed only five days in Palermo. Then, via a long detour, we went back to Taormina, which we both wanted to see again. Did I say that the village is perched high on a mountainside? The railway station is next to the sea. I had to take the coach that brought us to the hotel down to the station to collect our trunks. I stood up in the coach to talk to the driver. He was a little Sicilian from Catania, as beautiful as a line of Theocritus, resplendent, fragrant and delicious as a piece of fruit.

'*Com' è bella la Signora!*' he said in a charming way as he watched Marceline walk away.

'*Anche tu sei bello, ragazzo,*' I replied. And as I was standing so close to him, and couldn't resist, I drew him towards me and kissed him. He merely gave a little laugh.

'*I Francesi sono tutti amanti,*' he said.

'*Ma non tutti gli Italiani amati,*' I replied, laughing in turn . . . I looked for him in the days that followed, but couldn't find him again.

We left Taormina for Syracuse. We were retracing our footsteps from our previous journey, working back to the origin of our love. And just as on our first journey I progressed week by week towards full recovery, so this time round, as we moved further south, Marceline's health grew worse by the week. What aberration, what stubborn blindness, what deliberate folly made me convince myself, and above all attempt to convince her, that what she needed was more light and warmth? Why did I hark back to my convalescence in Biskra? . . . The weather was already a bit warmer; the climate of Palermo is very clement and Marceline liked it there. If she had stayed there, she might have . . . But could I determine my own will, could I decide my own desires?

We had an eight-day wait at Syracuse because of the rough seas and the irregularity of the boat service. Whenever I wasn't with Marceline I was down in the old port. Oh, little port of Syracuse! The smell of sour wine, muddy backstreets, the stinking market frequented by dockers, tramps and drunken sailors. I found the lowest types the most delectable company. I had no need to understand their language when I could feel it in my whole body. I misread the brutality of their passion as a sign of health and vigour. It was no use telling myself that their miserable lives would not have the same appeal to them as they did for me . . . Oh, I would have loved to drink myself under the table with them and not wake up until the first mournful shiver of dawn. In their company

I felt even more strongly my growing hatred of luxury, of comfort, of that protective blanket which my new state of health had rendered obsolete, of all the precautions one takes to insulate oneself from the hazardous contact with life. I tried to imagine their lives further. I would have liked to follow them further, probe deeper into their drunken lives . . . Then suddenly the image of Marceline flashed before my eyes. What was she doing at this moment? Suffering, crying perhaps . . . I jumped to my feet and ran back to the hotel, which might as well have had a sign above the door: 'No poor here'.

Marceline always greeted me in the same way – without a word of reproach or mistrust – and she always managed to smile in spite of everything. We ate our meals in private – I ordered for her the best this mediocre hotel had to offer. While we were eating I thought: a piece of bread, some cheese, a head of fennel is enough for them – that would be enough for me too. And perhaps there are others not too far away who haven't even got that meagre fare to assuage their hunger . . . And there is enough food on this table to feed them for three days! I wish I could have knocked down the walls and allowed some dinner guests inside . . . Knowing there were people out there starving was awful. And I went back down to the old port and distributed the loose change in my pocket at random.

Poverty makes slaves of men. In order to eat they will do work they hate. Any work that isn't joyful is wrong, I thought, and I was paying them so that they could rest. I told them, 'Don't work, you hate it.' I wanted to give every one of them all that leisure without which nothing new can develop – no vice, no creativity.

Marceline could see what was really going on in my mind. When I came back from the port, I did not hide the fact that I had been consorting with some low-life characters. Man contains everything. Marceline had an inkling of what I was relentlessly seeking to discover. And as I accused her of always believing in people's virtues that she herself had attributed to them, she said, 'But you aren't happy until you get them to display some vice. Don't you understand that when we fasten on to a particular feature in someone we tend to exaggerate it? And that we make that person into what we want him to be?'

I wanted to believe she was wrong, but I had to admit that it was always the worst instincts in people that seemed to me the most sincere. But what did I mean by 'sincere'?

We finally left Syracuse. I was obsessed by my memories of the south and my desire to return there. At sea Marceline felt better . . . I can still see the colour of the sea. It is so calm that the wake of the boat seems to stretch to infinity. I can hear the sound of dripping water: the swabbing of the decks, the slap of the sailors' bare feet on the planks. I can see the white outline of Malta, the approach to Tunis . . . How I have changed!

The weather is fine and warm. Everything looks splendid. How I wish I could distil, in each of my sentences, the essence of a whole harvest of voluptuous delight . . . It is no use trying to impose an order in my story when there was none in my life. I have been trying for some time to explain to you how I became what I am now. Oh, if only I could clear my mind of this insufferable logic! . . . I feel there is nothing in me that is not noble.

Tunis. The light is replete rather than strong. It even fills the shadows. The air is like a luminous liquid: everything seems to be soaking in it, people seem to swim through it. This land of pleasure satisfies desire without assuaging it; instead, desire is stimulated once more.

A land unencumbered with works of art. I despise those who can't see beauty until it is transcribed and interpreted. What is so wonderful about the Arab people is that they live their art; they sing it and dissipate it on a day-to-day basis. They don't preserve it, embalm it in works of art. This is both the cause and the effect of their lack of great artists . . . I have always believed that the great artists are those who dare to portray as beautiful a thing which is so natural that anyone seeing it afterwards would say, 'Why have I never noticed how beautiful this is?'

At Kairouan, which I hadn't been to before, and which I visited without Marceline, the night was very beautiful. As I was going back into the hotel on my way to bed, I remember noticing a group of Arabs lying out in the open air on mats in front of a small café. I slept beside them, and came home crawling with vermin.

The clammy heat of the coast made Marceline feel extremely weak. I convinced her that we needed to go to Biskra as soon as possible. It was the beginning of April.

ANDRÉ GIDE

It was a very long journey. The first day, we made it to Constantine
in one go. The second day, Marceline was very weary and we got only
as far as El Kantara. Towards evening we finally found what we had
been looking for: a shadow that was cooler and more delectable than
the moonlight. It was like an inexhaustible, refreshing stream flowing
towards us. And from the bank where we sat we saw the plain ablaze
with colour. That night, Marceline couldn't sleep – she was disturbed
by the strange silence and alert to the slightest sound. I feared that she
was a bit feverish. I heard her tossing and turning in bed. In the morning
she looked paler. We set off again.

Biskra! Let us move on to the end of our journey . . . Yes, here is
the public park, the bench . . . I recognize the bench where I sat during
the early days of my convalescence. What was I reading then? . . .
Homer. I haven't opened it since. Here is the tree whose bark I stroked.
How weak I was then! . . . Look, the children! . . . No, I don't recognize
any of them. How serious Marceline looks. She has changed as much
as I have. Why is she coughing, in this lovely weather? Here is the
hotel. Here are our rooms, the terraces. What is Marceline thinking?
She hasn't said a word. As soon as we arrive in our room she lies on
the bed. She is tired and says she wants to sleep a little. I go out.

I don't recognize the children, but they recognize me. Forewarned
of our arrival, they all came running. Can it really be them? What a
blow! What has happened? How they've grown, in barely more than
two years. It's not possible . . . their faces, once so bright and youthful,
already seem lined by toil and vice and sloth. What vile labours have
wrecked these fine, young bodies? Such ruin . . . I ask around: Bachir
washes dishes in a café; Ashour scrapes a living on the roads breaking
stones; Hammatar has lost an eye. Who would have believed it? Sadeck
has settled down; he helps his elder brother sell bread in the market;
he seems to have become a bit of an idiot. Agib has set up as a butcher
with his father; he has grown fat, ugly and rich and won't talk to his
old friends any more . . . How respectable careers make pigs of us! Am
I going to find the same things here I detested so much at home?
Boubaker? He got married. He isn't yet fifteen. It is grotesque. Well,
not quite. I saw him later in the evening. He told me his marriage is
just a sham. I get the impression he is an out and out rake. But he

drinks, lets himself go . . . Is that all there is left? Is this what life has done to them? I feel unbearably sad at the thought that it was them I most wanted to see again. Ménalque was right: memory is a product of unhappiness.

And what about Moktir? Ah, he has just got out of prison. He's keeping his head down. The others no longer have anything to do with him. I want to see him again. He was the most handsome of them all. Will he too disappoint me? . . . They find him and take me to him. No! He hasn't lost it. He looks even more splendid than I remember. His strength and beauty are simply perfect . . . He recognizes me and gives me a smile.

'So what did you do before you went to prison?'

'Nothing.'

'Did you steal?'

He protests.

'What are you doing now?

He smiles.

'Well, Moktir, if you have nothing to do, you will have to come with us to Touggourt.' I have a sudden desire to go to Touggourt.

Marceline is not doing so well. I don't know what is going on in her mind. When I get back to the hotel that evening she presses herself to me without a word, with her eyes closed. When her wide sleeve slides up I see how thin her arm is. I hold her and rock her as if she were a baby I am trying get to sleep. Is it love, anxiety or fever that makes her tremble so? . . . Oh, perhaps there is still time . . . Will I never stop? After much searching I have found the thing that sets me apart: a sort of stubborn attachment to evil. But how will I be able to tell Marceline that we set off for Touggourt tomorrow? . . .

At present she is asleep in the room next door. The moon is now high in the sky and is flooding the terrace with light. It is almost terrifyingly bright. There is nowhere to hide from it. My room has white tiles, and it is particularly evident there. It floods in through the wide-open window. I can see its brightness inside the room and the shadow that marks the shape of the door. Two years ago it penetrated even further – yes, it has almost reached as far as it did that night when I got up, unable to sleep. I leaned against the jamb of this very same door. The palms are motionless as they were then . . . what were the words I read that night? . . . Ah yes, Christ's words to Peter: 'When you were young, you girded yourself and walked where you would . . .' Where am I going? Where do I want to go? . . . I didn't tell you that when we were at Naples this time I went to Paestum on my own one day . . . Oh, I could have wept at the sight of those ruins! They stood in all their ancient beauty – simple, perfect, smiling . . . and deserted. I am losing my art, I can feel it going – to be replaced by what? Not, as before, a happy harmony . . . I no longer know the dark god I revere. O new God, show me new peoples, unimagined forms of beauty!

The next day at dawn, we leave on the coach. Moktir comes with us. Moktir is as happy as a king.

Chegga, Kefeldorh', M'reyer . . . dreary halts and an even drearier journey, which goes on for ever. I confess I had expected the oases to be more welcoming. But there is nothing but rock and sand, a few stunted bushes with strange flowers, the odd crop of palms, clinging on to some hidden source of water . . . I now prefer the desert to the oasis – a land of deadly glory and unbearable splendour. Here the work of man seems paltry and ugly. Now any other land bores me.

'You are in love with the inhuman,' says Marceline. But how she gazes at it herself! How avidly!

The weather worsens on the second day – the wind picks up and the horizon looks hazy. Marceline is in a lot of discomfort. The sand we inhale burns and irritates her throat, the excessively strong light hurts her eyes; this hostile land is killing her. But it is too late to turn back. We shall be in Touggourt in a few hours' time.

It is this last part of the journey that I have most trouble remembering, even though it was not so long ago. I am unable to picture that second day, or what I did when we reached Touggourt. What I do remember is how impatient and impetuous I felt.

It was very cold that morning. Towards evening, a hot simoom begins to blow. Marceline, exhausted by the journey, goes straight to bed as soon as we arrive. I hope to find a more comfortable hotel: our room is awful; everything is tarnished, dirtied and discoloured by the sun, sand and flies. As we have hardly eaten anything since dawn, I order a meal immediately. But Marceline can't face it, and I am unable to get her to eat a thing. We have brought the wherewithal to brew tea. I attend to this derisory fare and for dinner we make do with a few dry cakes and this tea, to which the dirty water hereabouts has imparted its disgusting taste.

By some vestige of virtue I stay with her until evening. Then all of a sudden I too feel at the end of my strength. O taste of ashes! O lassitude! The sadness of superhuman effort! I scarcely dare look at her. I know that instead of seeking her gaze, my eyes will gravitate with horrified fascination to those dark holes of her nostrils. Her expression of suffering is appalling. She does not look at me either. I can feel her anguish as well as if I were touching it. She coughs a lot, then goes to sleep. Every so often, she is shaken by a violent shudder.

This could turn into a bad night, and I want to know where I can find help before it gets too late. I go out. Outside the front door of the hotel the town square, the streets, the atmosphere itself are so strange I almost can't believe I am there seeing them. A few moments later, I come back in. Marceline is sleeping peacefully. I was worrying about nothing. In this weird land one expects danger everywhere – it is absurd. Sufficiently reassured, I go out again.

Strange movement on the square: silently, secretively, the white burnous glide by. Every now and again, the wind tears off a shred of strange music and whisks it in from who knows where. There is someone coming towards me . . . It is Moktir. He was waiting for me, he says, he thought I would come out again. He laughs. He knows Touggourt well, he comes here often and he knows where to take me. I allow myself to be led.

We walk in the dark. We go into a Moorish café – that's where the music was coming from. There are some Arab women dancing – if you could call that monotonous shuffling dancing. One of them takes me by the hand. I follow her. She is Moktir's mistress. He comes with us . . . We go into a deep, narrow room with nothing in it but a bed . . . a very low bed, where we sit down. We startle a white rabbit which has been locked in the room, but before long it is tamely eating out of Moktir's hand. We are served coffee. Then, while Moktir plays with the rabbit, the woman draws me towards her, and I succumb as one succumbs to sleep . . .

Oh, at this point I could deceive you or say no more, but what use is my story if it is not truthful? . . .

I return to the hotel alone; Moktir stays behind for the night. It is late. A dry sirocco is blowing – a wind full of sand and torrid even at night. After a few steps I am lathered in sweat. But I am suddenly in a hurry to get back and I am almost running when I return home. Perhaps she has woken up . . . perhaps she needs me? . . . No, the casement window of her room is dark. I wait for a short break in the wind before opening it. I enter very quietly in the dark. What is that noise? . . . It doesn't sound like her cough . . . I put on the light.

Marceline is sitting half on the bed. She has one of her thin arms wrapped around the bars of the bed, holding her upright. The sheets, her hands and nightdress are drenched with blood. It is all over her face. Her eyes are hideously enlarged. No cry of pain could have chilled me more than her awful silence. I try to find somewhere to plant a kiss on her perspiring face; the taste of her sweat lingers on my lips. I wash her forehead and cheeks . . . I feel something hard under my foot beside the bed. I reach down and find the little rosary that she asked me for back in Paris, which she has dropped on the floor. I place it in her open hand, but she drops her hand and lets it slide to the floor again. I don't know what to do. I want to find someone to help . . . She grabs me with her hand, desperately. Oh, does she think I want to leave her? She says:

'Oh, can't you wait a little longer?' She sees that I want to speak. 'Don't say anything. Everything is all right.'

I pick up the rosary again and put it back in her hand, but she drops it again – yes, she deliberately lets it go. I kneel down next to her and press her hand to me.

She falls back, half against the bolster, half against my shoulder; she seems to sleep a little, but her eyes remain wide open.

An hour later, she sits up again. She disengages her hand from mine, grabs at her nightdress, tears the lace. She is choking.

Towards morning, she vomits up more blood . . .

I have reached the end of my story. What else is there to say? The French cemetery in Touggourt is a hideous place, half engulfed by the desert . . . With what strength I had left I got her away from that miserable place. She lies in El Kantara, in a shady private garden she loved. All this happened barely three months ago. Those three months feel like ten years.

Michel remained silent for a long time. We too said nothing, we all shared a strange unease. We felt that, by telling us this story, Michel had somehow justified the way he had behaved. By not condemning his actions at any point during his long explanation, we were as good as being accomplices. We were in some way implicated. He finished his story without a quaver in his voice, without any sign of emotion, whether because he took some cynical pride in appearing impervious to feeling, or because he feared we might be embarrassed to show our own feelings in reaction to his tears, or because he actually felt nothing at all. Even now, I don't know in what proportions his attitude was attributable to pride, strength, tact and emotional sterility. After a pause, he continued:

The thing that scares me, I have to admit, is that I am still quite young. I sometimes feel as if my real life has yet to begin. Take me away from here and give me a reason to live. I no longer have one. Maybe I have liberated myself. But so what? I find this empty liberty painful to bear. It is not, I promise you, that I am tired of my crime, if you want to call it that, but I must prove to myself that I have not gone too far.

When you first knew me, I was very consistent in my thinking. I know that that is what makes a real man. I am no longer like that. But I believe that this climate is one factor. Nothing is more unhelpful to thinking than this unremittingly blue sky. It is impossible to make any mental effort here; pleasure follows so closely on the heels of desire. Amidst all this splendour and death, one constantly encounters happiness, and one invariably surrenders to it. I take a nap at midday to break up the intolerably long, dreary days of endless leisure.

You see those white pebbles over there? I leave them to cool in the shade, then I hold them in my hands until I have absorbed their soothing coldness. Then I start again with new pebbles, placing the warmed-up pebbles back in the shade to cool. The hours pass, evening comes . . . Take me away from here. I am no longer capable of doing it myself.

Something in me has snapped. I don't even know how I found the energy to get away from El Kantara. Sometimes I am afraid that the things I have suppressed will take their revenge on me. I want to start afresh. I want to get rid of what remains of my fortune – you can see it all over my walls . . . Here, I can live on next to nothing. A half-caste innkeeper prepares my food. The boy you saw running away when you arrived brings it to me every morning and evening, in exchange for a few sous and the odd caress. He is shy in front of strangers, but with me he is affectionate and faithful like a dog. His sister is an Ouled-Naïl who goes to Constantine every winter to sell herself on the street. She is very beautiful and in the first few weeks I was here, I allowed her to stay the night. But one morning, her brother, little Ali, found us in bed together. He was very annoyed and wouldn't come back for five days. Yet he knows how his sister makes her living – he used to talk about it, and it obviously didn't bother him . . . Was it perhaps that he was jealous? Well, at least the rascal has got his own way: half through boredom, half for fear of losing Ali, I haven't seen the girl again since that incident. She wasn't annoyed, but now every time I bump into her she laughs and teases me that I prefer the boy to her. She makes out he is the reason I stay here. Perhaps she is not altogether wrong . . .

FOR THE BEST IN PAPERBACKS, LOOK FOR THE ⟨🐧⟩

In every corner of the world, on every subject under the sun, Penguin represents quality and variety—the very best in publishing today.

For complete information about books available from Penguin—including Penguin Classics, Penguin Compass, and Puffins—and how to order them, write to us at the appropriate address below. Please note that for copyright reasons the selection of books varies from country to country.

In the United States: Please write to *Penguin Group (USA), P.O. Box 12289 Dept. B, Newark, New Jersey 07101-5289* or call 1-800-788-6262.

In the United Kingdom: Please write to *Dept. EP, Penguin Books Ltd, Bath Road, Harmondsworth, West Drayton, Middlesex UB7 0DA.*

In Canada: Please write to *Penguin Books Canada Ltd, 10 Alcorn Avenue, Suite 300, Toronto, Ontario M4V 3B2.*

In Australia: Please write to *Penguin Books Australia Ltd, P.O. Box 257, Ringwood, Victoria 3134.*

In New Zealand: Please write to *Penguin Books (NZ) Ltd, Private Bag 102902, North Shore Mail Centre, Auckland 10.*

In India: Please write to *Penguin Books India Pvt Ltd, 11 Panchsheel Shopping Centre, Panchsheel Park, New Delhi 110 017.*

In the Netherlands: Please write to *Penguin Books Netherlands bv, Postbus 3507, NL-1001 AH Amsterdam.*

In Germany: Please write to *Penguin Books Deutschland GmbH, Metzlerstrasse 26, 60594 Frankfurt am Main*

In Spain: Please write to *Penguin Books S. A., Bravo Murillo 19, 1° B, 28015 Madrid.*

In Italy: Please write to *Penguin Italia s.r.l., Via Benedetto Croce 2, 20094 Corsico, Milano.*

In France: Please write to *Penguin France, Le Carré Wilson, 62 rue Benjamin Baillaud, 31500 Toulouse.*

In Japan: Please write to *Penguin Books Japan Ltd, Kaneko Building, 2-3-25 Koraku, Bunkyo-Ku, Tokyo 112.*

In South Africa: Please write to *Penguin Books South Africa (Pty) Ltd, Private Bag X14, Parkview, 2122 Johannesburg.*